I've travelled the world twice over,
Met the famous: saints and sinners,
Poets and artists, kings and queens,
Old stars and hopeful beginners,
I've been where no-one's been before,
Learned secrets from writers and cooks
All with one library ticket
To the wonderful world of books.

© JANICE JAMES.

SIMON LASH
Private Detective

Private detective Simon Lash was far more concerned with his library of rare Americana than with the prospect of gaining clients, but when Joyce Bonniwell arrived one morning in a state of extreme agitation, there wasn't much Lash could do; after all, ten years ago he and Joyce ... Her husband, Jim, had disappeared. 'An attack of amnesia,' she said. But it wasn't, for out of the mountains came the news of the discovery of Jim's body; he was dead — murdered — and he wasn't the first to die.

Books by Frank Gruber
in the Ulverscroft Large Print Series:

THE TWILIGHT MAN
TWENTY PLUS TWO
BRIDGE OF SAND
THE GOLD GAP
THE BUFFALO BOX
MURDER '97

FRANK GRUBER

◆

SIMON LASH

PRIVATE DETECTIVE

Complete and Unabridged

ULVERSCROFT
Leicester

First published in the
United States of America

First Large Print Edition
published December 1995

British Library CIP Data

Gruber, Frank
    Simon Lash: private detective.—Large print ed.—
Ulverscroft large print series: mystery
I. Title
823.912 [F]

    ISBN 0-7089-3429-3

Published by
F. A. Thorpe (Publishing) Ltd.
Anstey, Leicestershire
Set by Words & Graphics Ltd.
Anstey, Leicestershire
Printed and bound in Great Britain by
T. J. Press (Padstow) Ltd., Padstow, Cornwall

This book is printed on acid-free paper

1

SLOCUM came into the library where Lash was sprawled on a couch reading a mint copy of *McClellan's Own Story*. He said:

"There's a client in the office, Chief."

Without looking up from his book, Simon Lash said, "No."

Unperturbed, Slocum continued, "She's wearing a mink coat that cost plenty."

Lash turned a page. "Let me alone, Eddie."

Slocum shrugged and went to one of the bookshelves. He looked at the titles for a moment, then took down a slender volume. Lash, whose eyes had rema'ned on his own book, snapped:

"Don't tell me you're learning to read Cherokee, Eddie?"

"Me?" said Slocum. "Uh-uh. I'm taking this Cherokee Bible down to Eisenschiml's."

At last Simon Lash put down his book. His eyes glinted. "What for?"

"Because the P & Q Grocery want their money. And the telephone company and the electric light company and the milk company want what's coming to them. I don't think Eisenschiml will give me enough on this Bible to cover it all. Shall I take the Lewis & Clark book along?"

Lash snarled. "Goddam you, Eddie!"

Slocum continued: "There's six dollars and forty cents in the bank. You haven't paid me my wages in over two months. The refrigerator is empty and there's nothing on the pantry shelf for me to cook. And you haven't worked in three months . . . "

Lash slammed shut *McClellan's Own Story*. "What does she want, evidence for a divorce? Even if we're starving we won't take a job like that."

"I think it's something more important, Chief," Slocum said. "She's scared stiff."

"Blackmail, eh? Well . . . what's her name?"

"I don't know."

"Ask her, goddamit!"

"I did. She wouldn't tell me. Insists

on talking to you personally."

"And she looks like money?"

Slocum nodded.

Lash swung his slippered feet to the floor and stood up. His trousers were unpressed, his shirt was tieless and his vest uncovered by suit coat. He needed a shave and his biweekly haircut was overdue. He was five feet ten and weighed one hundred and sixty pounds.

Slocum said, candidly: "You look like hell, Chief."

"Then tell her to go away. I wouldn't doll up for any woman."

Savagely, he stepped to the library door and jerked it open. There was a six-foot hall leading to the office and another door opening on it.

He opened the door, closed it behind him and — stopped.

He didn't see the mink coat. He saw Joyce Prentice — no, Joyce Prentice Bonniwell. She was sitting on the edge of a chair, facing him. Her face was pale, even through heavy make-up.

She said: "Hello, Simon."

Eddie Slocum had said she was frightened. Lash knew that it took more

3

than mere fright to bring her here. It had to be stark terror.

He thought of that . . . and it made no difference. It was ten years and for half of those years he had known that it would make no difference.

He walked to his desk, sat down in the swivel chair and swung around so he faced her. He said calmly: "Hello, Joyce."

By that time she was flaring at him, with her mouth slightly open. Her throat muscles contracted, her mouth opened wider, but she had to make a second effort to speak before words came out. And then they were inane, merely:

"It's been a long time, Simon . . . "

He nodded agreement. "My assistant said you wanted to see me — on a business matter."

Her eyes became normal and a slight shudder seemed to run through her body that was as slender as it had been ten years ago.

"Yes, Simon," she said, "I — I've heard of your work and . . . " Her words trailed off. She couldn't talk to him. It would have been hard enough if he had been as she had known him years ago. But now, impersonal and — cold — she couldn't bring out the words she wanted to say to him.

His eyes searched her face for a moment, then he said in a brittle tone:

"What is it — your husband? You want to divorce him and you need evidence?"

She flinched as if he had struck her. But his brutal words had the proper effect. Her nostrils flared and she snapped angrily:

"I've been very happy with Jim Bonniwell."

"Yes? Then why did you come here? I'm a detective . . . "

Her sharp white teeth bit into her lower lip. She worried the flesh a moment before replying.

"You didn't let me finish. I said I've been very happy with Jim Bonniwell. But . . . he's disappeared."

His lips twisted into a contemptuous curl. "Then why didn't you go to the police? The Bureau of Missing Persons? . . . "

She got up from the red-leather chair. Her face taut and pale, she said, "I'm sorry if I bothered you. I came to you with a delicate, personal matter because I — I thought you'd understand and you choose to deliberately insult me and — "

"Sit down!" His words crackled at her and he leaned forward across the desk. "Sit down and tell me what it's all about. If it's a matter I think I can handle, I'll do so. I am, after all, a licensed private detective. There are certain things I can do better than the police. On the other hand, ordinary missing person cases can be handled much more capably by the police department. I take it this isn't an ordinary case? . . . "

Her red tongue came out and moistened her lips. Then suddenly she seated herself again in the red-leather chair. "It isn't an ordinary case. Jim . . . has been subject to spells of amnesia."

"Amnesia?" Again his lips curled, but she refused to look at him. Fixing her eyes upon the edge of the desk, she went on:

"This is the third time he's been affected. The first time he was found wandering about Santa Monica in a dazed condition. When the police questioned him he did not even know his name. Fortunately, he had some letters . . . and they brought him home. He recovered quickly. The second time — "

"Just a moment! How long had he been missing the first time?"

"Two days. It was four days the second time. He recovered by himself then — in Phoenix, Arizona. He had no idea how he'd gotten there."

"And now?"

"He's been gone twelve days. And — he had tags with his name and address sewed into his clothing in case it happened again. He hadn't been feeling well at all lately and I was rather worried. In fact, I'd employed . . . " She hesitated, then shook her head in annoyance and plunged. "I'd employed a private detective to follow him . . . "

"Who?"

"A man named Burkhart. The Otis Agency furnished him. But Jim disappeared with Burkhart following him."

"How? I don't think much of the Otis Agency, but I happen to know Burkhart and he's a capable shadow."

"Burkhart couldn't say. Jim went into a café on Wilshire and Burkhart made the mistake of waiting outside. It seems Jim went right through the café and out by a back door."

Lash grunted. "Sounds as if he knew he was being shadowed."

"I thought of that. Burkhart claimed no."

"He would, naturally. Well, what do you want me to do?"

"Why . . . why, I want you to find Jim, naturally . . ."

"I'm not a magician. Or a mind reader. I know nothing about Bonniwell's business — or private — affairs. I don't know if he had any reason for wanting to disappear . . ."

"Wanting to disappear?" Joyce Bonniwell cried. "What do you mean?"

Lash scowled for a moment. "I never did like amnesia stories. A man's worried and harried by something he can't face, so he runs out. When he's discovered, he hollers, 'Amnesia' . . ."

"Do you have to be insulting, Simon?" Joyce Bonniwell said hotly. "Do you think it was easy coming — to you — and asking for your help? I *did* go to another detective agency first. They botched the job. And I'd heard from a friend that you were capable, even though eccentric."

"Eccentric? Who said that about me?"

"Julia Mainwaring. She said that you acted like a — a fiction detective. You don't go outside once a month; you spend all your time reading silly books . . . "

"All right," Lash cut in, "that's enough. My private life is my own. I don't accept every case that comes along, but when I do accept one, I give it everything I have. And I generally succeed. I'll be frank with you. I don't believe in amnesia. As long as you understand that, all right. I'll find your husband for you and you can fight it out with him yourself. Now, give me something to go on . . . What was Bonniwell worried about?"

"Worried? I don't know. He . . . seemed . . . I mean, what makes you think he was worried?"

"You wouldn't have hired a shadow if you hadn't suspected he was about to go off. He'd been acting strange again, hadn't he?"

"Yes. But it didn't seem to be worry.

9

He was absent-minded . . . vague. And a little afraid, I would say. He acted somewhat like that before the other times."

"He's a banker, isn't he?"

"Why, yes. He's a vice-president of the Sheridan National. And a director."

"Now don't bite my head off," Lash scowled. "Has Bonniwell been tapping the till at the bank? I mean, has he — "

"No," Joyce Bonniwell retorted. "Money has not been one of Jim's troubles. His income has always been quite adequate."

"That's fine. A good income is *important*." Lash made the emphasis almost an insult. "But we'll skip that. I've got to begin somewhere. I can't just go out into the street and yell, 'Oh, Jim Bonniwell; where are you?'"

"I realize that. But what information can I give you?"

"The names of his friends . . . and enemies."

"He has no enemies. And as for friends . . . his fellow club members, I suppose. The Sunset Athletic Club."

"What about relatives?"

"Not in California."

"All right — habits? Did he drink?"

"No more than anyone else, I imagine. He usually stopped in at the club for a drink before coming home."

"What about night clubs . . . and such?"

Lash, covertly watching, saw her chin come up a fraction of an inch. "No night clubs," she said, "except for once or twice a year, when we went out with friends." Her nostrils flared a trifle. "It seems to me you're approaching this from the wrong angle, if you think Jim — "

"No, no," he cut her off. "Not at all. I'm merely trying to establish Bonniwell's character. That's important. A man suffering from amnesia will do the things he would do in his normal life. Habit is subconscious. If Bonniwell patronized night clubs in his regular life, he'd be apt to do so in his amnesia condition . . . I want to know where to look for him . . . and I think I have enough now to begin."

She got up from the red-leather chair. "You'll get right to work?"

He nodded. "I have no other pressing

cases. Just one thing more: How far am I to go in incurring necessary expenses?"

"Why, as far as necessary. The main thing is to find Jim . . . soon. He'll need medical attention . . ."

"Of course. Well . . . suppose you mail me a check, for expense money . . ."

Again her nostrils flared and her color deepened. She opened her purse and brought out a wad of folded bills. She moved forward to Lash's desk and dropped the bills on it.

"Will five hundred be enough — for the time being?"

"It'll be quite satisfactory. I'll let you know when I need more."

He pushed back his chair. "Where can I reach you, to report progress?"

She gave him an annoyed glance. "Beverly Hills . . . of course!"

He was supposed to have known that. That he didn't showed a lack of interest in her affairs. He bowed and moved to the door with her. As she went out, he whirled to meet Eddie Slocum coming out of the dining room, a pad and pencil in his hands.

"Get it all, Eddie?"

Eddie nodded. "Including the five hundred. I better hustle that down to the bank so we can write out checks for the rent and — "

"Four hundred will be enough. We'll need the rest for immediate expenses."

2

T HE Sheridan National Bank was on Hollywood Boulevard. It had five tellers and two or three men on the other side of the banking room, who sat behind low railings and talked to people about loans and such things.

Mr. Vincent Springer, the president, however, had a private office. Simon Lash got in by the simple expedient of brushing past the uniformed guard who was loitering near by outside Springer's office.

Vincent Springer was in his late forties. He still had black hair and his face was a pleasant pink from countless massages and close shaving. He looked up from his desk, started to frown and then put on his best customer's smile.

"Did you want to see me?" he asked.

"Not necessarily," Lash replied curtly. "But since I've got to ask you some questions I suppose I'll have to see you."

The smile left Mr. Springer's face. "I don't think — " he began and then Lash cut him off.

"It's about Jim Bonniwell. I've been employed to find him. I'm Simon Lash."

Annoyance struggled with apprehension on Springer's face and was finally vanquished by an expression of suave blankness.

"Yes, of course," Vincent Springer murmured. "Shock to me as well as to his wife. You're representing Mrs. Bonniwell, I presume?"

"I'm working for her, yes. What can you tell me?"

"*I* tell you? Why, there's nothing I know. Undoubtedly Mrs. Bonniwell has told you that her husband was not a stranger to these attacks . . ."

"Phooey!" sneered Lash. "I don't believe in amnesia and neither do you. Not when it affects bankers. How much did he walk off with?"

Mr. Springer's pink face became a violent red. "What — what are you insinuating, sir?"

"I'm not insinuating anything; I'm asking. Did Jim Bonniwell tap the till

15

here, or did he just appropriate some of the customers' securities?"

Vincent Springer pushed back his chair and placed both hands flat on his polished desk. "Your remarks, sir, are not only ridiculous, but slanderous. It happens that Jim Bonniwell is my friend, as well as business associate, and I won't have anyone — "

"All right, all right," Lash snapped. "I apologize. Jim Bonniwell didn't abscond. You tell me then why he walked out?"

"He didn't walk out. He was ill. Mrs. Bonniwell . . . "

" . . . Told me all about his previous attacks of amnesia. I still don't believe them."

Mr. Springer's well-manicured right hand reached out and settled down upon a hand phone. "I think I'll call Mrs. Bonniwell."

"Go ahead," Lash invited. "I told her the same thing. She still wants me to find Bonniwell. How about — you?"

"Why, of course, I want to find him!" Springer cried. "Why shouldn't I? He's needed here in the bank and he's been gone two weeks . . . "

"I thought it was only twelve days?"

"Twelve days, more or less. It's too long, anyway. He never stayed away that long before."

"Why haven't you notified the police?"

Springer gasped. "The police? Why — why, that would be tantamount to a declaration that something *is* irregular . . . here, at the bank."

"And there isn't?"

"Of course not! Bonniwell will come back. It might be today."

"I doubt it," Lash retorted cynically. "But let that pass for a moment. What can you tell me about Bonniwell, personally? His character . . . "

"One of the finest," Springer declared emphatically. "A man of the highest character, absolutely above reproach."

"You ought to be in Philadelphia, nominating him," Lash said caustically. "I can see where I'm going to get nowhere fast."

"That's just about enough from you!" Springer cried furiously. "Get out of here."

"I was just going. But — I may be back later."

Lash turned on his heel and stormed out of the office, with Springer denouncing him.

Outside he climbed into the coupé, beside Eddie Slocum. "Just a waste of energy. Drive to the Sunset Athletic Club. We'll see what we can nose out there."

When he got out of the car in front of the Sunset Athletic Club building, Lash said to Slocum:

"Give me a minute to get inside, then tackle the doorman. Get to the bell captain and maybe one of the waiters on room service. You might pick up something that I'd miss."

"Okay, Chief."

Lash went into the club, nodding to the doorman. He had been a member once and the man still recognized him. In the lobby he saw the manager about to step into his office. Lash called to him:

"Mr. Plennert!"

The club manager turned. "Why, Mr. Lash, how are you? It's been a long time since you were here."

"Hasn't it? I'd like to talk to you a moment."

"Of course, Mr. Lash. Will you come into my office?"

Lash followed him into the cubbyhole that served as an office. Plennert crowded in behind a small desk and waved Lash to a chair. "You're thinking of coming back to the club, Mr. Lash?"

"No. I don't like exercise."

"Ha-ha!" laughed Plennert. "The exercise most of the members indulge in around here isn't very strenuous."

"I know the strain is on their bank accounts rather than their muscles . . . You know that I'm a detective?"

"I'd heard you'd given up your legal practice, but . . ." Plennert's eyes drew together. "If you're here in your professional capacity, why you know I couldn't reveal anything about the members. So many important men, you know . . ."

"Spare me the roll call. I know the stuffed shirts. Jim Bonniwell has had another attack of amnesia . . . "

"Amnesia!" exclaimed Plennert.

"You didn't know that Bonniwell gets attacks of amnesia? He loses his memory, then wakes up, maybe five hundred miles

19

away, walking the streets of Phoenix, Arizona, or drinking champagne in the Palace Hotel in San Francisco."

"Why, that's terrible! I had no idea . . . "

"Neither does he. He's off somewhere, now. Maybe in Portland, Oregon, maybe Albuquerque, New Mexico. I've got to find him."

"Of course, but how will you know where to look for him?"

"That's it. I don't. I don't even know where to begin. That's why I'm here. I want to find out who his friends were, learn his habits."

"Habits?"

"Uh-huh. Good, as well as bad, the idea being that he'd subconsciously do the same sort of things in his amnesia condition. What can you tell me about him?"

"Why, I only knew Mr. Bonniwell through his being a member of this club. I guess he does the usual things men in his position do. He plays a little poker, goes to the races and drinks . . . in moderation."

"What about women?"

Plennert looked annoyed. "This is an athletic club!"

"I know," said Lash, "I was a member. That's why I'm asking you; what about women? Did he take any to lunch or dinner here, did he get phone calls? . . . "

"I wouldn't know about that," Plennert said coldly. "Naturally we don't spy on our members."

"The hell you don't. Nothing happens in this club that you don't know about."

The club manager reddened. "Look here, Mr. Lash, I don't believe I care for this at all. You're no longer a member and — "

"And I'm a private detective. Would you rather I sent the police around to ask the questions?"

"The police!" gasped Plennert. "*Here?* . . . "

"Here. And they'd walk all through the lobby, into the card and billiard room, the Turkish baths — everywhere. They'd wear nice blue uniforms and they'd stop your important club members and ask *them* questions."

Plennert looked harassed. His forehead creased and he chewed at his lower lip with his teeth. "I don't get the idea of this at all, Lash. Is Mrs. Bonniwell seeking divorce evidence? . . . "

"I don't handle divorce cases. I told you Jim Bonniwell had disappeared and I'm trying to find him."

Plennert's eyes smoldered. "I still can't help you. I know nothing of Mr. Bonniwell's habits. He was no better or worse than any other member of this club."

"What did she look like?" Lash snapped at the club manager.

"I never saw her. It was — well, it was the mail. He got letters; baronial-style pink envelopes, heavily scented."

"Now we're getting somewhere. What was the name on them."

"That's it, there wasn't any."

"How often did the letters come?"

"Quite often, for a while. Four and five a week."

"You say a while? Did they stop coming?"

"Oh yes, he hasn't received any for a couple of months."

"That's just about the time he disappeared the last time. Look, Mr. Plennert, can I talk to your mail clerk?"

Plennert frowned. "What good would that do?"

"If he got so many letters, he must have written to her, too. And he undoubtedly mailed some of the letters from here. The clerk might remember to whom they were addressed."

The club manager began scratching the back of his neck. "The help's apt to be indiscreet. I wouldn't want gossip started about any member . . . "

"There won't be. You can threaten to fire him if anything gets out."

Plennert hesitated a moment, then reached reluctantly for his telephone. "Tell Myers to come into my office."

A minute or two later, a slender youth in his early twenties came into the manager's office. His hair was so oily Lash was surprised the oil did not drip off onto his face.

"Myers," said Plennert, "this is Mr. Lash. He wants to ask you something about one of out guests, something in the strictest confidence. If word gets about the club that you were even asked such a question — well, you know what to expect."

"Sure, Mr. Plennert." The mail clerk turned to Lash. "Shoot!"

"It's about James Bonniwell. I understand he received frequent letters in envelopes that were highly perfumed . . . "

Myers smirked. "That's right. A dame — "

"Don't jump to conclusions, Myers," Plennert said severely. "The letters may have been from Mrs. Bonniwell."

"That's right, maybe they was. Only it seems funny she'd write him even on Sundays when he would be at home . . . "

"Smart lad," murmured Lash. "Let's see what else you observed. What about Mr. Bonniwell's letters? Did he write many to any certain person?"

Young Myers shook his head. "That's what had me stumped for a while, but I finally figured that this was some dame who had a crush on him and she kept writing him and he never answered . . . "

"Never?"

"Not that I noticed. He might have mailed the letters outside."

"He might have. But did he mail other letters here?"

"Sure, a lot. He'd send packages now and then, too. But they wasn't for a dame."

"How do you know?"

"I got a good memory." Myers coughed. "Most of his correspondence was with a guy — a man, I mean. Fella named Loomis, Oscar Loomis."

Lash's eyes narrowed. "And this Loomis' address — you remember that?"

"Yeah, sure, it was on Wilshire, in West Los Angeles. A hundred and twenty-seven something or other."

"Or other, what?"

"I don't know. It had five numbers; one twenty-seven, maybe eighty-five or eighty-seven. Uh-uh, thirty-seven. Gosh, now I'm getting confused myself. It's quite a while, you know and — "

"Of course. I guess that'll be all, Myers."

After the mail clerk had gone, Plennert looked inquiringly at Lash. "Well, there doesn't seem to be anything unusual about Bonniwell's affairs. A woman pursued him, but apparently he didn't let himself be caught."

"Apparently, not. Well, I guess that'll

be about all." He nodded at the club manager and left the office.

In a corner of the lobby he saw Eddie Slocum talking to a bellboy. He gave him a signal and walked out. After a moment Eddie joined him at the car.

"What'd you get, Eddie?"

Eddie started the motor of the coupé and slipped out into the traffic of Sunset Boulevard. "Not much, Chief. He behaved pretty well around the club. Gambled maybe a bit steep, but if he's a banker he's pretty well heeled."

"What about his friends?"

"His best one was his boss, Vincent Springer, the president of the Sheridan National. Springer's a member of the club, too. Where to, now?"

"Wilshire, out toward Westwood."

Slocum turned left at Highland Avenue. Lash leaned his head against the back of the seat.

Not until Eddie Slocum had turned west on Wilshire and they were rolling through Beverly Hills did he speak: "Where to on Wilshire, Chief?"

"The hundred and twenty-seven block. We're almost there."

A few minutes later Slocum pulled over to the curb.

Lash got out of the car and looked up the street. "You take the other side, Eddie. We're looking for a man named Loomis. Oscar Loomis. You've got five houses over there, I've got three and an apartment."

"What do I do if I find him?"

"Nothing. Just let me know."

Eddie Slocum crossed the street and Lash turned toward the house nearest to him. On a hunch he passed up the house and the one next to it and advanced toward the California-style apartment house that sprawled over half the block. It had a typical California name, 'Casa Del Mar.' It was only three stories tall, but the apartments inside probably rented for from $150 to $200 a month.

He climbed a long flight of stairs and opened the front door. There was no desk inside the hall, but a sign over a door read: 'Office.'

He rang the doorbell. After a moment the door was opened a few inches by a woman in a bright-green wrapper, pulled tightly over protruding red pyjama trousers.

"Mr. Oscar Loomis," Lash said, matter-of-factly.

"He isn't here," replied the woman manager. "He's gone on one of his business trips."

"Darn," said Lash, putting real disappointment into his tone. "I was afraid of that. I'm his cousin and I've just run down from Seattle. Os wrote that he had to take a trip, but I didn't think he'd go so soon. When is he expected back?"

"He didn't tell me. Why don't you ask Mrs. Loomis?"

Lash blinked. "She didn't go with him?"

"She never does. Second floor, Apartment B."

Lash climbed the stairs to the second floor and proceeded to the door of Apartment B. He pressed the doorbell.

Inside the apartment a voice squealed. "Just a minute!" Lash could hear shoes pad on a rug, then the door was opened wide, by an astonishing creature.

She was no more than twenty-one or twenty-two and had the most flaming red hair Simon Lash had ever seen. He did not believe it could be natural, yet her delicate, pinkish complexion was that of a red-haired girl. She wore toeless shoes, sheer hose through which he could see red toenails and a pale-green frock of filmy organdie.

She was a dazzling bit of femininity, as she first stared at Lash. But then the light went out of her eyes and her face drooped. "Oh, I thought it was someone else . . . ," she mumbled.

"I'm looking for Oscar Loomis," Lash said.

"He isn't here," the girl replied and started to close the door. Lash moved forward so that the door stopped against his shoulder. "I know that," he said, "but I'm still looking for him."

Her eyes widened a little in apprehension. "What do you mean?"

"I mean, I want you to tell me where he is."

It was fright now in her eyes. She tried to push the door again, but he put his weight against it. Then suddenly he moved forward and let the door swing shut behind him.

She sprang back. "Get out of here! How dare . . . "

Lash smiled frigidly. "Would you prefer I brought a warrant?"

She gasped. "You're a — a policeman?"

He shrugged. "Where's Oscar Loomis?"

"I don't know. He's away on a business trip."

"Yeah? What kind of business?"

"Why, why . . . " she floundered. "Just business."

"What business is Mr. Loomis engaged in?"

She went back farther into the room, stopping with her shapely calves touching a modernistic chair. Lash made an impatient gesture. "Sit down, Mrs. Loomis. I want to ask you some questions."

She stared at him wide-eyed and he saw that her eyes were violet, which was quite in keeping with the rest of her vivid color scheme.

She sat down abruptly but was so tense that he could see her flesh quiver.

"Let's start at the beginning," he said, "you're not really married to Oscar Loomis, are you?"

The pink of her face became a flaming red. It went down her throat line. "Why, how dare you! . . . "

"Mrs. Bonniwell is looking for her husband," Lash said bluntly.

The red faded from her face as quickly as it had come an instant before. It receded until she was not even pink. Moisture came to her violet eyes.

"Mrs. Bonniwell . . . " she whispered.

"Uh-huh," he replied. "Oscar Loomis is really James Bonniwell. You knew that, didn't you?"

Her chin started to nod, stopped, then moved down again. But suddenly it came up and a ripple went through her. "All right," she said defiantly. "It's true, so what? But I don't know where Jim is. I — I've been nearly out of my mind waiting for him . . . "

"So has Mrs. Bonniwell."

The shot made her wince. Lash continued relentlessly. "How long since you've seen him?"

"Two weeks. He's never been away this long before . . . "

"You're sure about that two weeks? It couldn't have been, say, twelve days?"

31

"Why, yes. It was a week ago Sunday that I saw him the last time."

A week ago Sunday was only eleven days. Trying to conceal his eagerness, Lash said casually: "What time of the day was it?"

"Early morning. He — he left right after breakfast. He didn't say anything; I mean, he didn't tell me not to expect him back in the afternoon and I — well, I was caught completely by surprise, when he didn't show up."

"I can imagine," Lash said dryly. "You're sure you had no intimation of what he was going to do?"

"None at all. Other times . . . "

"What other times?"

Her sharp white teeth worried her lower lip. "He didn't stay here all the time."

"No. How often?"

"Just now and then. But he always told me when he was going away . . . "

"You knew he was married?"

Her eyes fell, giving him the answer.

An unreasonable anger seeped into Simon Lash. Anger not so much toward Jim Bonniwell, because he was a rounder, but at Joyce Bonniwell. She must have known — had some inkling at least — that Jim was playing around, on the side. Yet she had given Lash positive assurance that her life with Bonniwell was one long honeymoon. She'd put on a good act for him, too, the distrait wife whose anxiety was more for her ill husband than for herself.

This girl here had accepted Bonniwell for what he was. She knew that he was married, that Bonniwell went home to his wife. She knew that and had been content.

Lash sighed wearily. "Did Bonniwell confide in you? I mean did he tell you about his business affairs?"

"Oh, no," the girl said quickly. "I mean, I knew he was a banker, but one of the things he liked about me was that he could forget his business when he was here. I never asked him anything and he never told me anything. Except about the minks. He kind of joked about that. Said he was raising a mink coat for me."

Lash looked blankly at her. "I don't get it. Do you mean he was raising minks?"

"Oh, no, he wasn't raising them himself. Someone else did that. But he owned them."

"Where did he keep them? And who was raising them?"

"I don't know. I didn't ask. He said he might make quite a lot of money on them and he was going to give me whatever he made."

Lash shook his head. "I wonder if you'd mind looking through his papers and things? I'd like to get a lead on this mink business."

"I wouldn't mind," the girl said, "only there aren't any papers. He never brought anything here."

"Sure?"

"I'm as anxious to find Jim as you are, Mister," she said spiritedly. "Probably a lot more anxious, since he forgot something before he went away."

"What did he forget?"

"That last week was the first of the month and that one hundred and seventy-five dollars was due on this apartment."

"You're broke?"

She shook her head. "No. I'm not broke. I've got three dollars and forty cents. Why do you suppose I'm dressed right now? I'm going out to get a job. I can't wait any longer. Sourpuss, downstairs, is after the rent and if she chucks me out I won't even have money to rent a hall bedroom. Unless . . . you're sure that Bonniwell has really disappeared?"

He nodded. "Didn't he ever tell you about his amnesia spells?"

She looked blank. "What's that?"

"Amnesia. Loss of memory."

She laughed shortly. "Jim Bonniwell? You're kidding. There wasn't anything wrong with his memory."

"Maybe you're right. But Bonniwell's walked off. He forgot to tell his wife where he was going; he didn't tell the people at the bank and he didn't tell his club. Where did he go?"

"Maybe he went up to his mink farm?"

"But you don't know where that is?"

"I don't. Honest."

Simon Lash scowled. He went to the window, which overlooked the front stairs leading to the sidewalk, and saw Eddie Slocum leaning against a concrete pillar.

He turned back to the girl. "Look, I've

got to go now. I may want to talk to you, later. Don't let the sour — the landlady — put you out. Tell her you've heard from Bonniwell and that he's coming back before the end of the week. Stay right here . . . "

"Sorry," she said, "I may sleep here, but I've got to work. I'm going out to get a job today."

"All right. I can't prevent your doing that. Good luck. But don't move away from here. Not without notifying me, at least. The name's Simon Lash and here's my address." He fished in a pocket of his jacket and brought out a soiled business card, which he dropped on a coffee table.

She looked at the card. "Simon Lash. Say . . . you're the detective that was in the papers two or three months ago!"

Lash shrugged. "I never read papers. What's your name? Your real name?"

"Evelyn Price."

"All right, Evelyn Price, I'll see you again."

When Lash came out of the apartment house, Eddie Slocum advanced to meet him. "Don't look, now, Chief," he said, "but there's a ginzo across the street casing this joint. He was there when we showed up."

Ignoring Slocum's warning, Lash shot a glance across the street. A man seated in a flivver jerked his face away and buried it in an open newspaper that he had been holding.

"What the hell's the matter with you, Eddie?" Lash snapped. "That's Burkhart of the Otis Agency."

"I'll be damned," muttered Slocum. "Why, the chump's wearing a phony soup-strainer. I didn't think Otis would let one of his monkeys stoop to that. Shall I go over and buzz him?"

"No. Let him alone. We're going home."

"Huh? What for?"

"We're quitting."

"Quitting?" cried Eddie Slocum.

"No woman's going to make a fool out of me," Lash said savagely. "I told her I didn't handle divorce stuff and she gave me the amnesia crap. I didn't believe it, but I thought there might be another angle. There isn't. Stop at the bank and get the money and take it back to her."

"But we can't do that, Chief! Once we accept a case — "

"Take the money back," Lash gritted. "Take it back before I get mad. I walked into that love nest like the sappiest sap from Sap City."

Eddie sighed in surrender. "Okay, Chief, okay, you don't have to bite my head off. I'll take the money back to her, but I'll have to wait until morning. The bank's closed by now."

3

WHEN Slocum returned to the apartment on Harper, from his trip to the bank the next morning, he found Simon Lash in carpet slippers, sprawled on the library couch, reading a copy of *Quantrill & the Border Wars.*

"I got the money, Chief," he said tonelessly. "Shall I take it to her, or mail it?"

"Mail it, ·but call her on the telephone first and tell her we're quitting. We should have told her that yesterday, so she could hire some other Peeping Tom. Give her the Wilshire address, too."

Slocum went into the office to make the telephone call and Lash resumed his reading. He was just getting interested in the Baxter Springs massacre when Slocum returned.

"She isn't home."

Slocum went to the bookshelves. He took down the Cherokee Bible and the

39

Lewis and Clark book. Lash stood the Quantrill book on end beside the couch and got up. He went to a shelf, scanned the titles and took down a book.

"Tell Eisenschiml this King Strang Mormon book is worth a hundred dollars. The lot ought to fetch two-fifty. Don't take a nickel less than two and a quarter. The dirty crook'll charge three hundred to buy them back, later. That's enough profit for him."

"Two-fifty won't hardly cover the current bills," Slocum said steadily.

"Then take the McCoy Cattle Trade book!" snarled Lash. "And the Clay Allison book. Take any goddam thing you like, but get to hell out of here and let me read."

Slocum got the books, then paused long enough to deposit the four hundred dollars he had retrieved from the bank, on an end table, and padded out of the room.

Simon Lash threw himself down on the couch again and picked up the Quantrill book. He read the gruesome account of the slaughter of the Federal troops by the guerrillas, but was unmoved. After a while he hurled the book violently across the room and got up.

"Damn!" he muttered. "Why don't people let me alone? . . . "

He stalked out of the library, into the office, and was about to sit down in the swivel chair, when the telephone rang. He scooped it up.

"Yes?"

"Simon?" cried the voice of Joyce Bonniwell. "I've just received terrible news. Jim . . . is . . . dead!"

"I don't believe it!"

"I'm afraid it's true. The police — "

"The police? I thought they didn't know anything about his disappearance. You said — "

"They have just telephoned from Ocelot Springs. They say that Jim was . . . murdered . . . "

For a long moment, Simon Lash held his breath. Then he let it out slowly. "Where are you, Joyce? Eddie Slocum tried to get you on the phone only ten minutes ago."

"I just got in, when the phone rang and it was the sheriff of Ocelot Springs. They'd just found — the body. Simon, will you? . . . "

"Yes," said Lash. "I'll leave for Ocelot Springs immediately. Do they want you to come up and make the identification?"

"They have to hold it — for an inquest, so they said it would be better if I came up. They were pretty sure, however . . . "

"All right, drive over here. My man's out with the car and I don't want to wait for him to come back. I'll be ready when you get here."

He hung up the receiver and darted into the library. Kicking off his slippers, he shoved his feet into shoes and caught up his coat.

He saw the money Slocum had deposited on the end table and scooped it up. He was ready with an overnight bag when Joyce Bonniwell rang the doorbell.

He met her at the door. "Are you ready to go?" he said. "I've left a note with instructions for Eddie."

An olive-drab Cadillac stood at the curb. It was almost new. "Better let me drive," Lash said. "It's two hundred miles to Ocelot Springs. I'd like to make it before dark."

He walked around the car and got in

behind the wheel. He started the motor and shifted into second, zooming the car toward Hollywood Boulevard. At Hollywood he roared down into Laurel Canyon and took the hairpin turns up the canyon drive in high gear.

Ten minutes later he exceeded the speed limit going through North Hollywood and Burbank. At Glendale he turned north toward San Fernando and picked up Highway 7.

Within a half hour the Cadillac rolled down the easy mountain grades, into Antelope Valley. It was a straight run now, through the desert. Heat waves shimmered on the highway, making it look like a ribbon of water, rather than a road. Driving with the windows open, the hot wind buffeted them like the blasts of a furnace.

It was the worst time of the day for driving through the desert, but Simon Lash thought it just as well. It was too hot for conversation. Joyce Bonniwell sat beside him, her face averted. If he did not want to talk, neither did she. The road was so straight and flat that the powerful Cadillac zoomed along at better

43

than eighty miles an hour as effortlessly as it would have done fifty-five around Hollywood.

They were beyond Palmdale when Joyce Bonniwell suddenly spoke. "I lied to you yesterday, Simon."

"I know," he grunted. "When Eddie Slocum called you on the phone and you weren't home, it was to tell you that I was quitting."

"Quitting? Why? . . . "

"Because I'd found out that you'd lied. About your being happy with Bonniwell."

He heard her gasp. "What do you mean? I was happy with Jim."

"All right. You were happy."

"That wasn't what I lied about. It was about Jim not having any financial worries. He — I mean, there wasn't any money. Jim lost a lot in the stock market. He was pretty desperate for money and that's why — I'm sure of it — why he suffered the amnesia attacks."

"Oh, you're still sticking to the amnesia story?"

She exclaimed, "What's the matter with you, Simon? Must you bite my head off every time you open your mouth?"

"No," he said, "but you admitted to one lie. Why don't you come clean and tell me all of it? I'd know where I was at."

"But that *is* all. Everything else I told you is the truth. I — I lied about the money, because I didn't want you to think I was so poor . . . "

"Where'd you get the five hundred?"

"That was my own money. It's — just about the last of it. When it's gone, there isn't any more. Not now."

"What about insurance?"

"Must you go on?" she cried desperately.

"No, I don't have to. Not at all. A doctor would have to ask you questions. In my business, questions bring information. I'm trying to establish a motive, that's all."

"But I don't know. I've told you all that I know. Jim's been ill for a year. Worry brought it on. I don't see why you persist in trying to make out more than that."

"All right," he conceded. "Do you want the truth, or don't you?"

"Of course I want the truth. But — "

"But it isn't what you say. Jim

45

Bonniwell suffered no more from amnesia than I. I found that out in the couple of hours I worked yesterday. There's an apartment on Wilshire Boulevard, with the name Oscar Loomis — "

"What?" cried Joyce Bonniwell. "Oscar Loomis lives in San Francisco."

"Eh? There *is* an Oscar Loomis?"

"Of course. He's an intimate friend of Jim's. In fact, he was best man at our wedding ten years ago. But he only gets down to Los Angeles once or twice a year. He wouldn't have an apartment on Wilshire."

Lash sighed wearily. "You paid me for information. You said you wanted the bad as well as the good. All right, there's a woman in this apartment on Wilshire. She uses the name of Mrs. Loomis but admits that she isn't married to Loomis. She — " Lash stopped and shot a glance at Joyce Bonniwell. She was leaning back against the cushion, her face as stiff as if it had been chiseled out of Vermont marble.

He said: "Shall I go on?"

"Yes."

"That's why I wouldn't believe the

happy marriage angle. And the amnesia. Because the Oscar Loomis of Wilshire is Jim Bonniwell."

"You're sure?"

"Pretty sure. The girl admitted he was Bonniwell. In fact, she's written a good many letters to him at the club, under his real name."

"What's her name?"

He shrugged. "Evelyn Price. She's — that type."

"What else have you found out?"

"That's all. When I got that far I decided to quit. It looked like you hadn't played fair with me."

"Then why did you decide to go ahead — come up here, with me?"

"Because I saw that I was wrong. There was no place for murder in the other setup. And, there was a man from the Otis Agency watching the Wilshire Apartment. You? . . . "

She shook her head. "No, I discharged them, after that man Burkhart lost him twelve days ago."

"This was Burkhart. Otis doesn't go in for blackmail; at least I never heard of it. There must be another angle. What about . . . the bank?"

"No. Vincent Springer is as concerned about Jim, as I — was. They were close friends."

Lash lapsed into silence for a few minutes. Then he shook his head. "What about that mink coat you were wearing when you came to my office yesterday?"

"What about it?"

"Mink coats cost a lot of money."

"Mine cost four thousand dollars. It's two years old. Up to a year ago, Jim didn't worry about money."

"Meaning that the amnesia came after the money went?"

"Yes. I consulted a specialist and he said that amnesia was definitely the result of too much strain . . . and worry. Jim lost quite a lot of money."

"How much is a lot to you?"

"A hundred thousand, probably more."

Lash whistled. "On the stock market?"

"Most of it. Some of it the shrinkage of securities. Jim's salary at the bank didn't quite cover our expenses."

Lash thought not, considering Bonniwell's gambling at the Sunset Athletic Club and the apartment on Wilshire.

He said: "Now, tell me more about Bonniwell. I want to fix his character better in my mind."

"Why, you've seen him."

"Ten years ago," Lash replied steadily. "And we didn't exactly become chummy then. A man changes a lot in ten years."

"Yes," she replied significantly. "I guess Jim changed, too. He became older, more mature."

"He must have been crowding fifty."

"Fifty!" Joyce Bonniwell exclaimed indignantly. "Jim was only forty-three." She shot a sidewise glance at Lash, but his eyes were upon the straight road ahead.

"All right, forty-three," he conceded. "I'd thought him an older man, ten years ago. Go on, did he kick the cat around when he got mad?"

His irreverence for the dead stung her. She said bitingly, "His disposition was very good. He was a gentleman — always. He drank a little, played golf and went to his club. He went to Hollywood Park and Santa Anita during the seasons. He was a ten-dollar mutuel-ticket buyer."

"An average man," said Lash. "An

49

average man of the upper brackets. But you can't seem to come around to that one thing — Wilshire . . . "

She winced. "I know. That's so unlike him. I still can't believe it. After all, we were married ten years. You get to know a person in that time. And Jim Bonniwell wouldn't have an apartment like that. His pride wouldn't have permitted it."

"But they knew it at the club. The bellboys and stewards whispered it. The manager was aware and tried to cover up, like a club manager always does."

"I'm not denying it," Joyce said. "It's just that I can't believe it. It would mean . . . that I never knew the real Jim Bonniwell."

"That's possible. But I've got to know him. You say he didn't have an enemy in the world. Yet . . . he must have had *one* enemy, someone who hated him enough to kill him."

She was silent for a moment, then ventured, "Perhaps . . . it wasn't murder. You asked about insurance a while ago; there's quite a lot . . . "

"How much?"

"A hundred thousand dollars . . . "

"Whoa!" exclaimed Lash. "You're reversing yourself. You scoffed at the idea before. And I don't believe that. I know about the Wilshire apartment, and a man who'd go in for that wouldn't commit suicide . . . to give his wife a hundred thousand dollars . . . "

Joyce Bonniwell gasped. "You! — " she began, then bit off the rest.

She spoke no more until they reached the desert town of Mojave and then it was Simon Lash who broke the silence. "Would you like a cold drink?"

Her mouth quivered for a moment, then broke. "Yes."

He bought soft drinks and brought them in the bottles to the car. They sipped through straws, while the Cadillac wheezed and groaned, as the comparative coolness contracted the overheated metal.

Refreshed, Lash got into the car and drove onto the slab again. To the left the sun was dropping down to the Sierra Nevada range. He sent the car hurtling forward again, with the speedometer needle quivering above the eighty mark. The miles rushed past them.

4

THE Red Ball of the sun had partially dipped behind Mt. Whitney when a road sign said: 'Ocelot Springs, 12 miles.'

It was fantastic country. To the right was desert, to the left the green range of wooded mountains. Not so far from here was Death Valley, the lowest point in the United States; below sea level. And — to the left was Mt. Whitney, the highest peak in the Country; 14,501 feet above sea level. There was snow on the entire mountain range.

Simon Lash's face was thoughtful as he drove those last few miles. He had a strange feeling about this whole affair Why would Jim Bonniwell come away out here to the desert and mountains to meet his death? He was a city man. His interests were in metropolitan centers. Even if he were a victim of amnesia, his subconscious self would not bring him out here.

Ahead, Simon Lash saw a huddle of flat buildings. They rushed suddenly upon them and they were in the town of Ocelot Springs. He had time to glimpse a road sign at the edge of town, reading: "Ocelot Springs, Population 600," when they were in the town. He braked the car to ask directions, then saw a weather-beaten sign at the door of the shack just beyond, reading: 'Sheriff's Office.'

He stopped the car and got out. "Well, there we are," he said.

Joyce Bonniwell shot him a frightened glance. This was going to be an ordeal for her.

Lash said: "I'll go in and see if the sheriff's here."

He walked to the shack and stuck his head into the open door. A man with long mustaches had battered boots up on a scarred desk.

"Are you the sheriff?" Lash asked.

"Dep'ty," was the reply. "Sheriff's out on a case."

"The Bonniwell case?"

The boots came down and scraped the floor. "Hey? What you know about that?"

"My name is Lash. I brought Mrs.

Bonniwell. She's in the car outside."

"Fine!" exclaimed the deputy. "I been waitin' here for you. Sheriff Bucker said to bring you right out."

Lash led the deputy to the Cadillac. "Mrs. Bonniwell, this is the deputy sheriff . . . "

"Joe Bull, Ma'am. Shore sorry 'bout what happened. 'Spect you want to run right out to the ranch?"

"What ranch?" Lash asked.

"Why, the mink ranch where it happened."

Simon Lash inhaled softly. "Mink ranch?"

"Yeah, sure, it happened out on Ben Castlemon's Mink Ranch. That's right out here, a couple miles, up on the mountain. I'll just step in the back . . . This's shore a fine car, Ma'am."

Deputy Bull climbed into the tonneau and leaned back luxuriously. "Turn left there at the crossroads and follow the road right up. Watch the turns, they're pretty sharp."

Simon Lash got into the car and headed it for the graveled crossroad. He turned left and almost immediately began to climb. After a quarter of a mile the gravel simply ran out and from then on the road was the natural dirt.

They climbed a thousand feet in the first half mile, then ran fairly level in a semicircle about a hill for hundred yards or so before starting another ascent, even steeper than the first.

"I asked Ben Castlemon once why he had his ranch so high up," Joe Bull offered in explanation. "Said it was on account of the climate. The higher up, the colder; and the colder, the better the pelt, he said. His place's eight thousand feet up and she shore gets cold there, 'specially in the wintertime."

Lash scarcely heard the loquacious deputy. His full attention was required for the road, which was nothing more than a series of hairpin turns, going upward continually. He hoped no car would be coming down, for the passing would be rather close. There was a sheer drop on his side of hundreds of feet.

They were almost at the very top of the mountain when Lash saw the ranch. It consisted of a weather-beaten frame house, a half-dozen sheds and a few wire pens, through which a little stream seemed to run.

There was a huge, white sign outside the place, on which was painted in foot-high, black letters: 'Castlemon's Mink Ranch.'

The sign seemed to be the newest thing about the ranch. Three or four dusty cars stood in front of the ranch house. A man who had been sitting on the door stoop got up when Lash stopped the Cadillac.

"Mrs. Bonniwell?" he asked.

"She shore is," Joe Bull replied. He got out of the car. "Where's Clarence?"

The man in front of the house turned and yelled at the top of his voice: "Clarence! She's come! . . . "

After having seen the deputy, Joe Bull, Simon Lash half expected the sheriff to be a real old-timer. He was pleasantly surprised. Rucker was no more than thirty, a lean sunburned man, six feet tall. He came out of the house and approached the Cadillac.

"How do you do, Mrs. Bonniwell?" he said in a crisp voice.

Joyce Bonniwell nodded. "Is . . . he . . . here?"

The sheriff shook his head. "No, Dr. Boyle has taken the body down to the village. I'd like to talk to you here, however."

"Of course," Joyce Bonniwell said with dignity. "I shall be glad to answer any questions you wish to put. This is Mr. Lash."

Sheriff Rucker turned steel-blue eyes upon Lash. "Would the name be Simon Lash?"

Lash nodded. "Yes, I'm a private detective."

"I know," said Rucker. He came over and shook hands. "I've heard of you. You're representing Mrs. Bonniwell?"

"That's right. Do you mind if I look around?"

"Not at all. Like you to, in fact. Mrs. Bonniwell, will you come into the house?"

Joyce Bonniwell shot a quizzical glance at Lash as she went into the house with the sheriff. The moment she was out of sight, Lash turned to Deputy Bull.

"Is Ben Castlemon around here, d'you suppose?"

"Let's go see. Be about feedin' time

57

for the minks now, I 'spect."

They circled the house and met a well-built man of about forty. He was coming from a series of low sheds near by and carried a galvanized bucket in either hand. He wore overalls and a Stetson hat.

"Hi, Ben," Joe Bull greeted. "Shake hands with Mr. Lash. He's a detective from the city."

Ben Castlemon shook hands without enthusiasm.

"So Rucker brought in help from the outside? There wasn't any need of that. He's making too much of this."

"So far I don't know just what happened, Mr. Castlemon," Lash said. "Mind giving me a few facts?"

"There's mighty few facts I know. Bonniwell came up here last week. He sat around moping most of the time and this morning when I came in from feeding the stock, there he was, with his head blown off."

"Do you mean that literally? His head blown off?"

"Just about. A 12–gauge shotgun does a lot of damage. It's as sure a way of committing suicide as I know of."

"Suicide?" asked Lash.

"Yes, of course."

Lash turned casually toward the deputy sheriff. Joe Bull's face was relaxed.

"Suicide?" Lash repeated sharply.

Castlemon blinked. "That's what I said."

"I thought it was murder . . . "

"Murder?" gasped Castlemon. "What you talkin' about?"

"When Sheriff Rucker telephoned Mrs. Bonniwell, he told her that her husband had been murdered."

"He's crazy!" cried Castlemon. "It was suicide. Why — it's plain as — Jeez! the gun was right by him on the floor, and his shoe was off . . . "

"One shoe or both?"

"Just the one. The sock too. The other shoe and sock was on. Good Lord! what was Rucker thinking about to make a statement like that? Welker said that Bonniwell was down in the dumps and — "

"Welker? Who's Welker?"

"Leon Welker. My partner."

"Is he here?"

"Of course. He's in the house with Rucker. Say . . . "

Whatever he was going to say remained unsaid. Sheriff Rucker opened the rear door of the ranch house and signaled to Lash. "Mind coming inside, Mr. Lash? Perhaps you'd better come, too, Castlemon."

They trooped into a kitchen where unwashed dishes stood on an oilcloth-covered table. Just beyond was the living room, or 'parlor,' a rather large room, furnished with rundown mohair furniture.

The room contained, besides those who had just come in, Joyce Bonniwell, a suave, slender man of about fifty with waxed mustaches, and a man in a dirty, white linen suit, who needed a shave.

"Mr. Welker," Sheriff Rucker introduced, nodding to the suave one, "and George Fly, our county attorney."

The county attorney shook hands. Welker merely bowed. Then Ben Castlemon burst out:

"Look here, Clarence, what's this about murder? You know durn well it was suicide and — "

"Oh no, Ben," replied the sheriff. "It was murder, all right."

"But it couldn't have been. He put the gun to his head and pushed down the trigger with his big toe — "

Joyce Bonniwell exclaimed. "Don't! . . . "

"Maybe you'd better finish feeding your minks, Ben," Sheriff Rucker said grimly. "Sorry, Mrs. Bonniwell."

Castlemon scowled and left the room. The sheriff turned to Lash then. "Mrs. Bonniwell has told me about her husband's amnesia attacks. Mr. Welker, on the other hand, insists there was nothing wrong with Bonniwell."

"I didn't insist," Leon Welker cut in. "I said he seemed considerably agitated, quite unlike his usual self. You put words into my mouth, Sheriff."

"Oh, did I?" Sheriff Rucker asked pleasantly. "This afternoon, too?"

Welker curled up his fingers and studied the well-manicured nails. "I told you I couldn't understand Bonniwell's actions. Since Mrs. Bonniwell has mentioned his attacks of amnesia a lot of things that seemed strange become clear suddenly. The more I think of it,

61

the more I'm convinced that Bonniwell *was* suffering from amnesia. Yes, it's the only explanation for his actions."

"And it's also a very good explanation for *your* explanation," Rucker said ironically.

"Not at all," said Leon Welker. "Bonniwell's de — loss — is a great blow to me. Unless . . . " He glanced at Joyce Bonniwell.

"I don't know what you mean," Joyce Bonniwell declared. "This is the first I've heard about Jim being interested in minks."

"You didn't know he was one of the owners of this mink ranch?" the sheriff asked.

She shook her head. "He told me nothing about it."

"That's odd," said the sheriff, "considering that he's been coming up here for the last year."

"How often?" Lash interposed.

The sheriff shrugged. "I didn't know him myself, but I've heard that he came up here two or three times."

Lash said to Leon Welker, "Just how was Bonniwell interested in this ranch?"

"He was the president."

"It's a corporation?"

"Not exactly. Call it a partnership. Bonniwell put up the money."

"And you?"

Welker showed a nice set of teeth, too even to be his own. "I was the sales manager."

"And the brains?"

"Well, Castlemon handled the stock; Bonniwell was inactive, so I guess you might say I was the brains of the firm."

"In what sort of shape is the — the firm?" Lash asked. "Financially, I mean."

Welker looked at Lash and put his tongue into his cheek. "The D.A., sheriff?"

"No," replied Rucker. "Mr. Ely is the county attorney. Mr. Lash is representing Mrs. Bonniwell. He's a private detective from Los Angeles."

"Oh, I see." Welker smiled, but made the smile an insult. "Am I under arrest?"

"I haven't said so. Do you object to answering questions?"

"Not if *you* ask them, or Mr. Ely. Of course if you've asked the city dick to help you . . . "

"I haven't," snapped Sheriff Rucker.

63

"But his ideas sound all right to me. I was about to ask you the same questions. Just what sort of shape was this business in?"

"Very good."

"What do you mean by good?"

"We were making money."

Sheriff Rucker frowned. "We're getting nowhere fast. I think perhaps it would be better to go down to Ocelot Springs to continue this. It's gotten dark outside."

"At your service," flashed Welker, not quite concealing a triumphant note in his voice.

Sheriff Rucker turned to his deputy. "You hold down this end, Joe . . . Understand?"

"You mean, keep an eye on Ben? Or you want him down with you?"

"He'd better stay here. Luke will stay too. The rest of us can go down."

It was pitch-dark when they got outside the ranch house and Simon Lash grimaced as he thought of the hairpin turns going down the mountain.

"I'll lead the way," Sheriff Rucker offered. "But you better stay in gear."

He went to his car and switched on the lights. By their beams Simon Lash led Joyce Bonniwell to her own Cadillac. When they had got in he started the motor and turned the car around. Sheriff Rucker meanwhile worked his own car into the road and blinked his lights to signal that he was ready to lead the way.

Lash followed the sheriff's car into the narrow road. Joyce Bonniwell spoke then. "I don't understand it, Simon."

"What?"

"Jim owning a mink ranch. He's the last man in the world I'd have expected to go in for something like that. His interests were exclusively urban."

"You told me your coat cost four thousand dollars, didn't you? That's the answer. There's big money in minks. Or there should be."

What he was thinking was that Jim Bonniwell had not taken his wife into his confidence . . . and he had told the Price girl about his mink venture.

5

THE hazardous descent down the mountain occupied all of Simon Lash's attention for the next few minutes. Beside him, Joyce Bonniwell sat with her feet braced against the floor boards.

When they finally rolled into Ocelot springs, she said, "Whew! I hope I don't have to make that trip again."

Lash said, "There *must* be money in minks for a man to live up there."

As they got out in front of the sheriff's office, he said to Joyce Bonniwell, "I want to make a phone call to Eddie Slocum, my assistant in Hollywood. Tell the sheriff I'll be along in a few minutes."

He walked across the street to a two-story building, which had a neon sign in the window, reading: 'Hotel.' Entering, he got $5.00 worth of quarters at the desk and went to the telephone booth at one side of the lobby.

He called the operator and in response

to her request fed three quarters into the slot. The call was put through inside of a minute and he heard Eddie Slocum's voice exclaim:

"Chief, what the devil you doin' way out in the desert?"

"Haven't got time for that, Eddie," Lash replied crisply. "Did you get the information I asked you to try for in my note?"

"Yes and no. I pumped Burkhart but he said the agency was called off the job less than an hour after we quit. But here's the pay-off. Their client was Vincent Springer, president of the Sheridan National Bank. That's the same outfit that — "

"Yes, yes, I know," Lash snapped impatiently. "Bonniwell's bank. Why did Springer call off the Otis Agency? You should have known I'd be interested in that . . ."

"Burkhart didn't know. I tried to follow the thing up myself, but I couldn't get to Springer. He's out of town."

"How could he be out of town if he called off the agency?"

"He called them off yesterday. Here's

another screwy angle to this business; when I got all through I thought just for the hell of it, I'd give the Price girl a buzz. She didn't answer the phone so I buzzed the landlady. She said the Price girl checked out last night."

"Damn!" swore Lash. "We missed up there. Mm, maybe Burkhart followed her after she left Wilshire. Try and contact him again and check on that . . . and here are a couple of things I want you to get on right away, late as it is. Take down these names: Leon Welker, Ben Castlemon. They're partners in a mink ranch that Bonniwell was interested in. You may not get much on Ben Castlemon. I think he sticks out here. But you might. Welker ought to be known in Los Angeles. He's a slicker. Try the better hotels and night spots until you get a lead on him."

Eddie Slocum groaned. "That's a heluvan assignment. I'll need two-three fellows to help with that."

"Get them, if you have to. But not from Otis. Try the Statman outfit. And then call San Francisco long distance and have the Claypool agency dig up what they can on a man named Oscar Loomis. He ought to be a big shot up in 'Frisco. Got that all?"

"Yeah. Welker, Castlemon and Loomis. Anything else?"

"Yes. See if you can't get to some employee of the Sheridan National. Someone not very important. A teller, maybe. Get his opinion of both Bonniwell and Springer."

"You mean if they've been tapping the till?"

"If they have, they've covered it so no mere teller will find out. But just on general principles . . . a heart-to-heart opinion. And you might try once more at the Sunset Club, since you know now for sure that Bonniwell was keeping this Wilshire redhead on the side. If I'm not back in town by morning I'll give you another ring. Get busy, Eddie."

"Sure, sure. You don't think I'll have much time to sleep with all the work you've given me?"

Lash hung up and the operator immediately rang and demanded an additional dollar and a half for overtime. Lash dropped the quarters in the slot and stepped out of the hot telephone booth, just as the drab county attorney, George Ely, entered the hotel.

"Uh, hello, Mr. Lash," he said. "The sheriff sent me over to ask you to come to his office."

"I was just coming." He fell in beside the county attorney and they left the hotel. As they started to cross the street, Lash said casually, "The sheriff's a pretty smooth worker. That was nice the way he discovered Bonniwell had been murdered."

"Uh-huh," replied the county attorney. "I figured Ben Castlemon for it myself, but Clarence seems to think Ben wasn't smart enough for a stunt like that."

"It was quite a stunt, wasn't it?" Lash kept his face averted, but his ears were attuned to pick up the county attorney's reply.

George Ely almost fell into the trap; almost. He began, "That gun had me fooled, but Clarence saw — " Then he stopped and shot a covert glance at Lash.

That was all. They reached the sheriff's office and entered. "I've been waiting for you, Lash," Sheriff Rucker said.

"I had to make a telephone call."

"To Los Angeles?"

Lash grunted and after waiting vainly for him to reply, Sheriff Rucker shook his head. "Mrs. Bonniwell has been telling us of Mr. Bonniwell's previous attacks of amnesia."

"That's right," said Lash. "The first time the police found him wandering the streets of Santa Monica. The next time he had an attack he came to in Phoenix, Arizona, and didn't know how he got there . . . "

Rucker seemed disappointed. "Is it your opinion then that Bonniwell came up here in an amnesia condition?"

"Not having seen him recently I couldn't say," Lash replied curtly. "I should think the people who saw him upon his arrival would know if he seemed dazed."

"He was dazed all right," chimed in Leon Welker. "He talked about all sorts of nonsense when he came out to the farm. Ben and I thought he'd had too much to drink. In fact . . . he got into a crying jag once." He looked quickly at

71

Joyce Bonniwell's frowning face. "Least, that's what we thought, but now that we know about the amnesia, it's clear — "

"Yes, yes," Sheriff Rucker cut in. "You said that out at the ranch." He turned to the county attorney. "George, suppose you could take Mrs. Bonniwell over to make the identification?"

Ely did not seem very happy at the suggestion, but agreed. "Guess I could, Clarence. Uh . . . you're not coming?"

"No, some other matters to take care of. Mrs. Bonniwell, will you go with Mr. Ely?"

"Of course." Joyce Bonniwell rose from the sheriff's swivel chair. Lash started to the door with her, but Rucker reached out and took his arm.

"Mind?" he smiled. "Like to talk privately to you."

Lash shrugged.

Leon Welker looked inquiringly at the sheriff. "You still want me to hang around?"

"No, but I'd suggest you check in at the hotel. I'll probably want to talk to you tomorrow."

"Fine. Don't care about going back

to the ranch tonight, anyway. See you tomorrow, then."

With the departure of Ely, Mrs. Bonniwell and Welker, Rucker walked leisurely around his desk and plopped down in his chair.

"All right, Lash," he said, "shoot."

"Where's the target?"

"Right here. Tell me what you know about Bonniwell."

"Uh-uh," said Lash. "You tell me what you know about him."

"That's not much. This is a small town and the mink ranch came in for some gossip, naturally. Particularly with a man like Ben Castlemon running it."

"Castlemon's a local?"

"Yeah. And he never did anything very startling before. When I was a kid he had a hardware business here in town. He lost that and started a garage. When that petered out he opened a filling station. Before he went into the mink business he was a bartender in one of the roadside cafés, one of the smaller ones."

"But he got back into the money?"

"It was a seven-day wonder. Bailey,

73

our local banker, told me that the outfit once had twenty-five thousand dollars on deposit at the bank. Which is a lot of money for Ocelot Springs."

Simon Lash glowered at the sheriff. "Where'd they get such money? I got a glimpse of the layout and they haven't got more than a couple or three hundred minks out there."

"They sell off the surplus constantly. Anyway, mink pelts are worth a lot of money. So I hear. I wouldn't know myself."

Lash rubbed his chin with the back of his hand. "Any way of your finding out just how much money the mink outfit has cleared through the bank in the last two years?"

"I could ask Bailey."

"Why don't you?"

"Maybe I will. Now, give me the lowdown on Bonniwell, from the Los Angeles angle."

"He was vice-president of the Sheridan National Bank."

"I could get that from the papers. I'd like the real dirt on him. How'd he get along with his wife? I mean . . . how come she came out here with a private detective?"

"I'm an old friend," Lash said steadily.

Rucker looked at him thoughtfully. "You came with her as a friend instead of detective?"

"Let me ask you one question, Sheriff. Why did you tell Mrs. Bonniwell over the phone that her husband was murdered, when you let the locals believe that he had killed himself?"

Bucker thought about that for a while, then nodded. "All right; Bonniwell's head was just about blown off. A double-barreled shotgun lay on the floor beside him and he had one shoe and sock off. Clear so far, isn't it? He put the muzzle against his face, then reached with his toe to push down the trigger . . . Ever see the kind of damage a shotgun does at close range?"

"Not on a man," Lash said, "but I can imagine."

"You can't until you see what happened to Bonniwell. You can be damn sure Bonniwell didn't shoot himself twice."

Lash gave a start. "Eh?"

"Both barrels were fired. You might

say that he touched both triggers with his toe; in fact, that's the theory Mr. Leon Welker suggested. I didn't contradict the theory, but I took a look around the room. The shotgun was loaded with regular bird shot and at the extremely close range, the charge stayed pretty close together. Not many of the shot missed Bonniwell, but some did and they went into the floor."

"The floor? He must have done it lying down."

"Ah," exclaimed Sheriff Rucker. "Now, you're coming to the point. Lying down, yes. Then how do you account for the fact that there are a half-dozen buckshot in the wall, a good five feet above the floor?"

Simon Lash inhaled softly and the sheriff nodded. "It's a cinch that he didn't fire one shot lying down, then get up and finish the job. So . . . it's murder."

Lash took a quick turn about the sheriff's office. Suddenly he whirled upon him. "Then it's got to be either Castlemon or Welker."

"Sure, but which one?"

"Arrest them both. If one did the killing the other is an accessory after the fact."

"That's not good enough. We don't split the law that fine, up here. I'd never get a conviction with a split ticket. One man is all they'll convict at a time. But which one will I toss them?"

"That's your problem," Lash said.

"That's why I haven't made an arrest yet. I've got to be sure. And . . . there's still the possibility that it might not have been either Mr. Welker or Castlemon." The sheriff suddenly gave Lash a sharp look. "That's why I wanted to talk to you . . . about Mrs. Bonniwell."

"No," Lash said. "Mrs. Bonniwell was in Los Angeles this morning. All morning. You talked to her on the phone yourself."

"I talked to someone who said she was Mrs. Bonniwell. Voices sound strange on the phone. But lacking proof otherwise, I'll take your word that she was in Los Angeles. Now who, besides Mrs. Bonniwell, will vouch for you, Lash?"

Lash grinned icily. "I thought you were getting around to that."

"Well?"

Lash didn't get a chance to answer. There was a heavy step outside the office and a man opened the door. "Is this the sheriff's office?" he asked.

"It sure is, Mister," Rucker replied. "Anything I can do for you?"

"Why, yes," said the newcomer. "I came here to see a friend of mine and asking for directions to his place I received the shocking information that he committed suicide, this afternoon."

Sheriff Rucker suddenly pushed back his chair. "James Bonniwell? You're a friend of his?"

"Yes, I was to meet him here today. My name's Loomis, Oscar Loomis!"

Simon Lash stiffened. His eyes went to the sheriff's face.

"Yes," Rucker said slowly. "I'm sorry to say that Mr. Bonniwell was killed this afternoon . . ."

"Killed? I thought? . . . "

"It was murder."

Oscar Loomis reeled back and the color drained from his face. He was a man in his early forties, somewhat fleshy, but still in good physical condition.

"Murdered!" he breathed. "Good Lord! . . ."

"You say you were to meet Mr. Bonniwell here?" the sheriff asked quietly.

"That's right, he telephoned me long distance yesterday. He said it was extremely urgent . . ."

"What was urgent?"

Loomis' eyes were still wide. His tongue came out and moistened his lips. "Why, he was in somewhat of a difficulty and asked me to help him out."

"What sort of difficulty?"

Loomis hesitated a moment, then shook his head. "I suppose I'll have to tell — now."

"That's right; it's a murder case."

"Well, it was financial. He told me he needed twenty thousand dollars at once and he asked me to loan him the money."

The sheriff's eyebrows formed peaks. "And? . . ."

"What do you mean?"

"What did you tell him; yes or no?"

"Why, yes. Jim was my closest friend. We were roommates in college."

"Umm," said the sheriff. "Well, how

79

were you going to loan him this money?"

"Why! . . . " Oscar Loomis reached suddenly into his inside breast pocket. He brought out a thick manila envelope. "Why, like this. Cash. It was urgent, so I brought it up."

Sheriff Rucker stared at the envelope. "There's twenty thousand dollars in that?"

"Of course. He needed the money right away, so I brought it up."

"From where? Los Angeles?"

"No, San Francisco."

Simon Lash said suddenly, "Mrs. Bonniwell is here."

Oscar Loomis wheeled on Lash. "Joyce *here*?"

"She's making the identification. In fact, I think that's her coming right now."

It was. Joyce Bonniwell came into the sheriff's office with the county attorney trailing her. She said: "It was — " then saw Oscar Loomis. "Os!" she cried. "When did you get here?"

"Just now, Joyce!" Loomis replied. He stepped forward and took both of her hands in his own. "This is terrible, Joyce!

I spoke to him only this morning . . . "

"You said yesterday," Simon Lash corrected.

Oscar Loomis shot Lash an annoyed glance. "It was last night, but this morning, too. He telephoned me around two A.M. I had to wait until nine before I could get the money . . . "

"What money?" Joyce Bonniwell cried.

Oscar Loomis winced. "I wasn't supposed to tell you about that, but — "

"Go ahead, Mr. Loomis," Rucker said.

Loomis scowled. "Well, it was just that Jim was temporarily short and wanted to make a small loan."

"Twenty thousand," said the sheriff.

Simon Lash's face loosened. The sheriff was a man after his own heart.

6

IT was approximately nine thirty, when Oscar Loomis made his surprise entrance on the scene. From then until midnight Sheriff Rucker's investigation whipsawed back and forth. Simon Lash, for the most part, remained out of it, but he sat by and listened.

When the sheriff finally called it a day, the net sum of Simon Lash's knowledge was pitifully small. He knew that James Bonniwell had invested heavily in the mink enterprise, that he had come out to Ocelot Springs two or three times during the past year, the last time the evening before.

Leon Welker had arrived at the ranch earlier and had made two or three trips down to Ocelot Springs. The only surprising information that came out, surprising as far as Lash was concerned, was the actual time of Jim Bonniwell's death. The partners had stayed up late the night before. They had held a business

82

meeting and either during the meeting or shortly afterwards, Bonniwell had made his phone call to Oscar Loomis in San Francisco, asking for the urgent loan.

That was the last time either Welker or Castlemon had seen Bonniwell alive. The last time to which they would admit. Welker himself had slept rather late in the morning. When he had finally got up he had gone out to where Castlemon was already working around the mink pens. He had talked with him a few minutes, then climbed into his car and gone down to Ocelot Springs. He had returned after a couple of hours and since it was then already noon and Bonniwell had not made his appearance, he had asked Castlemon about it.

Castlemon had informed him that he had been too busy with his work to bother about Bonniwell. But now, the two partners decided to see what was keeping Bonniwell in bed so late. They had gone to his bedroom and had found him on the floor, fully dressed, but practically decapitated by the shotgun blast. They had immediately telephoned the sheriff.

That was all they would admit. In a half day's questioning, before Simon Lash had appeared upon the scene, Rucker had been unable to obtain further admissions from the pair.

They had had a meeting the night before. Yes, there had been some heated discussion. No quarrel, merely discussion. What had they discussed? Business details, that was all. The firm was in good shape financially. They insisted on that. And they knew of no reason why Bonniwell should at the end of their discussions telephone his friend, asking for a large loan.

That was the gist of the thing. And with it, Simon Lash finally retired to a room at the Ocelot Springs Hotel. He undressed and stretched out on the bed, but could not sleep and after a while dressed and went down to the lobby again. He utilized some of the quarters he still had to telephone to Hollywood, but the operator was unable to get Eddie Slocum, proof that his little assistant was making an all-night job of it.

Lash was annoyed, but reflected that he had insisted on Slocum sticking to the job and finally, shrugging, went back to his room and to bed.

* * *

He was out of bed and dressed a few minutes after six and, shivering in the morning chill of the desert, went down to the hotel lobby. Joyce Bonniwell's Cadillac was standing outside the hotel.

He crossed the street and went into a restaurant. A couple of natives at the counter were discussing the 'news,' which apparently was a sensation in this isolated community.

"If you ask me," one of the natives was saying, "it was one o' them city gangsters that knocked him off."

"Nah," the other retorted. "What would gangsters be doin' 'way out here? It was a woman, that's what I say. D'you see the one says she's his wife? She's even better-lookin' than the one he brung out here with him."

Lash came up behind the man and tapped him on the shoulder. "What did she look like, the woman he brought out?"

The native swiveled about on his stool and, looking into Lash's grim face, recoiled.

"Uh . . . who?" he mumbled. "What you talkin' about?"

"You were making some comment about a woman James Bonniwell brought out here with him?"

"Bonn'well? Who's he?"

"The man who was murdered here yesterday. That's who you were talking about."

"Naw, we wasn't talkin' about him," protested the native. He appealed to his companion. "Was we, Yancey?"

Yancey winked bleary eyes at Lash. "Nah," he said.

Lash glowered and went to one of the tables. He had scarcely seated himself than the two natives got up from their stools, dropped money on the counter and departed from the restaurant.

A waiter wearing a ketchup-stained apron came to take Simon Lash's order. "What were the names of those men who just left?" Lash asked.

The waiter shook his head. "Don't know them. What'll you have?"

"Ham and eggs, the eggs well done. And some coffee." Simon Lash glared at the retreating figure of the waiter. He was an outsider and these people here would stick together.

The door of the restaurant opened and Leon Welker came in. The 'brains' of the mink firm looked at Simon Lash, hesitated, then beamed. "Good morning, Mr. Lash," he greeted. "Mind if I join you?"

"I don't own the joint," Lash snapped.

Leon Welker chuckled and pulled out a chair opposite Lash. He sat down. "Glad to get a chance to talk to you, Lash. I haven't got much faith in the yokel sheriff. He's approaching the thing all wrong."

"Is he? In what way?"

"Why, trying to make something out of Bonniwell's death."

"Oh, you don't subscribe to the murder theory?"

"Of course not. It's ridiculous."

"Sure," said Lash. "It's ridiculous, because it points the finger at you."

Welker bared his teeth in a grin, but there was no humor in it. "That's one reason, but it's not the best one. I'm going to tell you another — and if you quote me to the sheriff, I'll deny that I said a word to you. Jim Bonniwell was a bank cashier. Catch on?"

"No," said Lash. "I don't. He was a wealthy man. If you're hinting — "

"I'm not hinting. I'm shouting it out loud. That's what our squabble was about. Bonniwell was broke. Dead broke. He wanted the firm to give him some money. Ben and I outvoted him. Twenty thousand taken out right now would have strapped us."

"I see," said Lash. "I see that you've heard about Oscar Loomis, showing up with twenty thousand dollars."

"That's right. We wouldn't give him the money, so he phoned Loomis. That verifies my statement."

"Does it? If Loomis was going to lend him the money, his troubles were over. He didn't have to commit suicide."

Welker screwed up his mouth. "Well, since you've got to have it, here it is. Bonniwell needed fifty grand and he needed it bad. As far as the business was concerned, that was out of the question. He tried to get thirty thousand from us, then came down to twenty. He figured that and the money from Loomis would give him forty thousand, and I guess he thought that would help him out of his hole."

"Suppose I were to tell you," Lash said deliberately, "that Bonniwell had thirty thousand in a safe deposit box in Hollywood?"

Leon Welker stared at Lash. He started to make a retort, then the waiter came up with Lash's order. Welker put in his own order, orange juice, toast and coffee. When the waiter had gone, he shook his head.

"I don't get you, Lash. Who're you working for in this?"

"Bonniwell's wife."

"That's what I thought," Welker declared. "Well, if you are, why don't you stay on that side?"

"I am. You haven't got a chance in the world of making the suicide theory stick, so better get yourself a new story."

Welker regarded Lash for a moment with parted lips. Then he said: "The

89

sheriff's got something! He told you — "

"You wouldn't try to pump me, Welker?"

"Why not? You're working for Mrs. Bonniwell and if it isn't suicide she's not in the clear."

The waiter brought Welker his meager breakfast. The mink man put the glass of orange juice to his mouth and drained it without taking it from his lips. He glowered at Lash even as he drank.

Lash speared the last bit of egg and finished his coffee. He pushed back his chair, then paused. "By the way, Welker, how'd you ever get a man like Bonniwell to go into the mink business with you?"

"Why not? It's big business. Have you got any idea how much a mink skin is worth . . . and how many mink a single pair will produce in a year?"

Lash laughed sardonically and moved toward the counter to pay for his breakfast. When he received his change, his head swiveled involuntarily to look back at Leon Welker. The mink man was hunched over the table.

Lash shook his head and went out of the restaurant.

Outside, the hotel clerk called to him from the middle of the street. "Oh, Mr. Lash, I was just looking for you. They say it's important."

Lash went into the hotel and entered the public booth in the lobby.

"Eddie?" he snapped into the mouthpiece.

"Yeah, Chief. I've been working all night. Just got in a minute ago and — "

"All right, all right, get to the point. What'd you find out?"

"I got some things, but I don't know what they're worth. First of all, I can't contact Vincent Springer. He lives out in the Palisades and I cased his joint myself. If he's home he's hiding down in the cellar — and I don't think they've got a cellar. What do you make of that?"

"How do I know? I haven't had time to think about it. What else? Did you reach one of Springer's Slaves?"

"Yeah. I got his name from the night watchman and looked him up. I found him in a poolroom and won eighty cents from him playing pool. He says Springer and Bonniwell were thick as thieves. Even went out on binges together."

"I knew that before. What about — wait! They make a habit of these binges?"

"From what this teller says. He took his girl to The Grove one time and there was Springer and Bonniwell with a couple of dizzy blondes and they weren't their wives."

"Check on that today, Eddie. Find out if that was just an expression — the blonde part. I want to know if one of them mightn't have been a redhead. All right, what about the rest? The bank part. Was either one of them dipping into the drawer?"

"Not as far as I could find out. The guy turned green at the very thought of that. But carrying through on Springer: I got Burkhart again. Springer didn't give any reason for calling off the job on the Wilshire redhead. But I couldn't run her down. Burkhart followed her down to an employment agency — "

"Employment or booking?"

"Well, I guess you might call it booking, but it's a dump. It was closed, of course. I'll try to find out today if she registered and if they have I'll get her address. It may cost me five bucks or so. Okay?"

"Okay, if you get the address. Now, what about San Francisco? Did you hear from Claypool?"

"Yeah, but not much. They hadn't made contact with Oscar Loomis. It seems he's out of town, too . . . "

"I know that!" cried Lash. "He's up here. But didn't the fools get anything on him? Who is he — what does he do?"

"I'll read you the wire, Chief. Here it is. 'Oscar Loomis out of city. Substantial citizen. Will give case history tomorrow. Air-mail check for one hundred.'"

Lash swore with feeling. "If they don't get more than that on Loomis they can sue me for their fee. Dammit all. What else did you get? Anything on Welker or Castlemon?"

"Nothing on Castlemon. A man named Welker stayed two days last month at the Hollywood-Wilson Hotel. They didn't know anything about him."

"Keep trying on him. Uh — you might even ask at the Sunset Athletic Club, to see if he wasn't a guest of Bonniwell's some time . . . "

"Fine. Which reminds me, I went back to the club and almost got thrown out by the snotty manager. He caught me pumping the bellboys. One of them's practically working for the agency, now. He says Bonniwell was one of the worst. He guzzled too much and the other members didn't care for him, but the bank has a mortgage on the club."

"Oh, so that's it. All right. Now, listen, Eddie I'll be coming home some time in the afternoon. By the time I get there I want to have a couple of real leads. I want a minute-by-minute report on Mrs Bonniwell for yesterday, beginning with the time she got out of bed in the morning — no, take that back to Six A.M; she might have got up early. And I want that redhead's address. She's important. And I'd like some dope on this Welker lad. And if there's no worthwhile information from the Claypool agency by ten o'clock on Loomis, I want you to call old Deacon Jones in 'Frisco. He's got a small agency, but does a little blackmailing on the side, so he's got to be good on digging up the dirt on somebody. Got that all?"

"Yeah, Chief, but I dunno if I can hold out. I'm all in . . . "

"From one night's work? If I come home and find you pounding your ear, you'll go back to touting at Hollywood Park. Now, get busy!"

He banged the receiver onto the hook and grabbed the door of the booth. He could not shove it open immediately because Sheriff Rucker was leaning against it from the outside. The sheriff grinned and stepped back so Lash could get out.

Lash snarled: "Listening, eh?"

"Uh-huh. I forgot to tell you that I also got a shorthand transcription of your talk with this Slocum last night. I tipped the operator to listen in. She's my sister."

Lash's eyes began to glow. "Why, you whistle-stop Keystone cop! . . . "

The sheriff held up his hand. "Hold it, Lash! You may be big stuff in the city, but this is Ocelot Springs. A murder was committed here and I'm the law. Come and sit down over here."

Lash's lips were a thin, straight line as he walked to one of the worn leather chairs in the lobby by the window looking

95

out upon the street. He threw himself down on the chair. Rucker seated himself carelessly in an adjoining chair.

He took a slip of paper from his pocket. "Vincent Springer, I gather, was Bonniwell's boss at the bank. He's the president of the Sheridan National Bank, a pretty sound bank from all I've ever heard of it."

"I didn't say it wasn't," Lash retorted.

"No, but you're wondering. You seem to think Bonniwell was an absconder. I've just had breakfast with Bailey, our own banker. He knew Bonniwell by reputation; said he's been with the Sheridan National for twenty years, starting as a teller."

"Regular Horatio Alger stuff," Lash sneered.

"Isn't it?" Rucker said calmly. "You know, after my sister gave me the transcript of your long-distance call last night I got an idea and put in one myself. To the police department in Los Angeles. I asked them about you."

"And they told you they'd never heard of me?"

"On the contrary, they knew quite

a lot about you. They said you were rather — er — unorthodox, but that you usually succeeded with the cases you handled."

"I'll remember that the next time I get a traffic ticket," Lash said sarcastically.

"They told me something else about you," Sheriff Rucker went on. "Something interesting. About your having been a promising young criminal lawyer eight or ten years ago."

A frown came to Simon Lash's face. "If you're finished I'd like to go and get my breakfast."

"You just had it — across the street. Listen to the rest. They said you gave up practicing law when the girl to whom you were engaged threw you over and married someone else."

Lash got up abruptly, but Sheriff Rucker finished quickly. "The man she married was named Bonniwell!"

His face twisted angrily, Lash glowered down at the sheriff. "I've got a business back home; if you're not going to arrest me, I'd like to get back to it."

"You can go any time, Lash," Rucker said, rising to his feet. "In fact, I figure on running down to the city myself some time today or tomorrow."

"Look me up when you get there," Lash snapped. "Look me up and I'll barbecue a moose for you." He stepped around the sheriff and walked toward the stairs, leading to the second floor of the hotel.

At the top he met Joyce Bonniwell coming out of a room, directly across from his own.

"Good morning, Simon," she said soberly.

"Morning," he replied shortly. "Better get your breakfast. I'd like to start back inside of an hour."

"An hour?" exclaimed Joyce. "Will the sheriff let us? . . . ."

"Yes, he's down in the lobby right now. Tell him you want to go home."

Lash went into his room and paced the floor for ten minutes. Then he went down to the now deserted hotel lobby. The clerk was cleaning his teeth with dental floss.

Lash approached the desk and, glancing at the hotel register, saw that a fresh page was showing.

"Let me see the register for the day before yesterday," he said to the clerk.

The man took the dental floss out of his mouth. "Can't."

"Why not?"

"'Cause the sheriff's already got it."

A bit of grudging admiration for the sheriff seeped into Lash. "All right, what was the name the woman used who came in with James Bonniwell?"

"Can't tell," was the reply. "Sheriff made me promise."

Exasperated, Lash took a five-dollar bill from his pocket. "Will that make you forget your promise?"

"Uh-uh," said the clerk, "but ten bucks might."

Lash gritted his teeth, but brought out another bill. The clerk waited until he had stowed the bills into his pocket. Then he chuckled. "Mrs . . . was her name."

Lash cursed. "Why, goddam you, give me that money back!"

"Keep your shirt on, Mister," retorted the clerk. "I'll give you your money's worth. It wasn't this Mrs. Bonniwell at all. She was nice-lookin', though. I figured her first for a movie actress. She was a blonde."

"You're sure? She didn't have a red hair?"

"Uh-uh, she was a real blondy kind of blonde. Pretty young, too, to be married to a guy as old as Bonniwell . . . Of course I didn't know then that they wasn't married."

"When did she check out?"

"She didn't. I mean there's three dollars still owin' the hotel for her and Mr. Bonniwell's room."

"You mean she just walked out of her room and disappeared?"

The clerk shrugged. "They checked in around six in the evening. Ben Castlemon was here waiting for Mr. Bonniwell. The three of them chewed the rag awhile, then Bonniwell registered for him and his wife — I mean, the woman. She went up to the room and Bonniwell went out to the mink place with Castlemon. Mrs . . . I mean, her, stayed up in her room for about a half hour, then came out and had supper across the street. I was just going off duty then — I work from seven in the morning to seven in the evening — when she came out of the restaurant. I saw her climb into her car. That's the last anyone ever saw of her . . . "

"What kind of a car was it?"

"I didn't notice. A good one, maybe a Buick. I didn't pay any attention to the license number."

"If you had," said Lash, "you'd be richer by another ten bucks."

"Well, that's the breaks," the clerk said philosophically.

Lash went to one of the chairs by the window and sat down to watch the restaurant across the street. After about ten minutes, Joyce Bonniwell came out with Sheriff Rucker. Rucker left her on the sidewalk to go to his office near by, and Joyce came to the hotel alone.

Lash got up.

"Are you ready to go now?" he asked when she came in.

She nodded. "Yes. Sheriff Rucker is going to take care of — of the arrangements. I'll just run up and pack my bag."

Lash went upstairs with her, but getting

his own bag went down to the lobby to wait for her.

Five minutes later, Lash looked sourly at the road sign, which read: "You are leaving Ocelot Springs."

7

JOYCE BONNIWELL said: "I can't understand it at all. My whole world seems to be falling around me."

Lash kept his eyes on the road ahead. He was always uncomfortable when persons about him were emotionally disturbed. He felt so little emotion himself.

"First Jim, then Os Loomis," Joyce went on. "He stayed at our house so often. I thought I knew him like a brother . . . and I didn't know him at all."

"Bonniwell seemed to know him well enough," Lash offered. "Well enough to borrow twenty grand." He was aware that her eyes were on him. He was silent for a moment, then sniffed disdainfully.

"Minks!"

Joyce took it up from there. "That's another thing that has astonished me. I never in the world dreamed that Jim was financially interested in a mink farm. Why, I remember one time — it was years ago — when he came home with that funny cat-and-rat farm story. He laughed himself sick about it; told it to a dozen people."

"I never heard that story," Lash said, more to keep Joyce in a lighter mood than from any desire to hear a funny story.

She laughed shortly. "It wasn't much, just one of those fantastic stories that sounds almost plausible. Something about having two farms, one for raising cats, another for raising rats. You feed the rats to the cats, then skin the cats and sell the skins and feed the cat carcasses to the rats." She shuddered. "It's really a horrid little story. The minks reminded me of it . . . somehow; they're such rattish-looking animals, really."

"Yet," said Lash, "coats made with their pelts cost four thousand dollars."

She grimaced. "I'll probably never wear that coat again, thinking of those minks."

"You can buy plenty of other fur coats . . . now," Lash said brutally.

She gasped. "Simon! Why! . . . ."

"I'm biting again, eh? Well, it's true,

isn't it? You were broke and the money will come in handy and it isn't as if — as if you had been still happily married — "

Her right hand came across in front of her and slapped his face. Fury put weight into the blow.

Lash finished, " . . . happily married," then took his foot off the accelerator and began applying the brakes. When he brought the car to a Stop, he said, "Good-bye," and climbed out.

Her face was white with anger. She slipped over behind the wheel, shifted into gear, and the big Cadillac jerked away.

Lash began walking. In three minutes the car was out of sight. As he swung along the pavement, his eyes glowed and his jaws were clenched so tightly; bunches of muscle stood out.

Ten minutes later a dusty, battered touring car drew up alongside of Lash. "Lift, Mister?" shouted a whiskered man in overalls.

Lash climbed into the car.

"Jeez," said the Good Samaritan, "you shouldn't ought to try hitchhiking out

105

here in the desert. Towns're too far apart and when the sun gets going . . . "

"I know," said Lash, "but I was expecting the bus to come along. I'm not broke."

"Then whyn't you wait back in Ocelot? Bus's due right now. How far you goin'?"

"Mojave, and I'd appreciate if you'd signal the bus when it comes."

"I'll do that, 'cause I'm only goin' up here to the borax works fifteen-twenty miles."

The bus came along in a few minutes, a hulking, zooming monster of gray. Lash's benefactor was compelled to block the road and signal frantically before the bus driver stopped blasting the desert with his horn.

They were nearing Mojave when Lash, looking out of the window saw the olive-colored Cadillac swishing past, going north. Her anger had held for a long time. He wondered if she would guess that he was aboard the bus when she would be unable to find him along the road. Well, the way this bus was rolling along the desert highway, he would probably be back in Hollywood before she was, considering the time she was now losing.

They got in at ten minutes to two and Lash took a taxicab out to Hollywood. When he entered the apartment the place smelled of stale food. Dirty dishes were piled up in the kitchen.

Lash swore feelingly, then got out a frying pan and some eggs. He let his dishes stand where he finished with them. Eddie Slocum would have a job when he got in.

He went to the library and for the first time in many hours relaxed. This was the only place where he really ever lived; during the hours when he lost himself in his hobby, the study of American frontier history.

This library represented a considerable investment. All the books were considered 'Americana' by collectors and book dealers and as such most of them enjoyed the additional appendage of 'rare.' Lash received the catalogues of every rare-book dealer in the country. He was one of their best customers.

His eyes roamed over one of the shelves, trying to decide with which volumes he could part with the least qualms, for it had come down to that. He would have to return Joyce Bonniwell's fee, in full, and he had already incurred considerable expense in her behalf. Eddie Slocum would howl, of course, but then Eddie always protested when Lash wasn't driving him and himself also, on some case. It wasn't the money with Eddie, as much as the zest of the chase, for when Lash had been flush on occasions, Eddie Slocum had to be reminded to take his salary.

The front doorbell rang as he was studying the books. Lash went to the door and discovered that it was a telegraph boy. He signed for the message, gave the boy a dime, and ripped open the envelope as he walked to his office.

The telegram was from Deacon Jones of San Francisco. It read:

OSCAR LOOMIS ADVERTISING MANAGER FOR RESTAURANT PROFITS, A TRADE JOURNAL. SALARY FIVE THOUSAND YEAR. FAR AS CAN DETERMINE NO OTHER INCOME. UNMARRIED. LIKES WHISKY, WINE AND WOMEN. EMPLOYER SAYS EXPENSE

ACCOUNTS EXORBITANT BUT LOOMIS
GOOD SALESMAN. WHAT ELSE DO YOU
WANT? THIS WILL COST YOU FIFTY. WIRE
MONEY AS AM BROKE.

DEACON.

Lash crumpled the telegram into a ball
and threw it into the wastebasket. He
turned to go back to the library and the
doorbell rang again.

It was another messenger boy. The
telegram this time was from the Claypool
Agency. It read:

LOOMIS EARNS MODERATE SALARY AS
SALESMAN. BELIEVED BY EMPLOYER TO
HAVE PRIVATE INCOME. SUBJECT OF
IMPECCABLE CHARACTER. NOT A BOOZER.
AT PRESENT OUT OF TOWN ON SELLING
CIRCUIT. PLEASE RUSH ONE HUNDRED
DOLLARS AS PER PREVIOUS REQUEST.

CLAYPOOL AGENCY.

Lash cursed and threw the telegram
after the first one. This time he did go
back to the library and he was sprawled
out on the couch reading *The Kansas
Crusade*, by Eli Thayer, when Eddie

109

Slocum came in, a half hour later.

Eddie exclaimed when he saw Lash. "Jeez, Chief! What're you doing, reading?"

"I like to read," Lash snapped at his assistant. "Any objections?"

"No, of course not, but — uh, aren't you working on the Bonniwell case?"

Lash gritted his teeth. "No, we're off it."

Eddie Slocum reeled back. "Again? For the love — "

"We got fired!" Lash snarled. "Now, shut up and let me alone. Here — " he reached into a pocket and brought out all the money he had left — "take this and put enough to it from what you got on the books to return the five hundred retainer."

"All right, but you told me to go ahead and hire Claypool and Deacon in 'Frisco. They'll want their money whether or not we — "

"Send it to them. See if I give a damn. Then get out there in the kitchen and clean up the mess you left. Nothing ever seems to get done when I'm not around here."

Eddie had scarcely left the room when

Lash heard the telephone ring in the office. But Eddie did not call him. Lash guessed that it was Joyce Bonniwell calling.

He read a page in his book, then got up and returned it to the shelf. He scanned further titles and finally took down Lowe's *Five Years a Dragoon*.

The new book was also a failure. Lash let it fall to the floor and stared, unseeing, at the ceiling. He had been doing this for years. His cases were few and far between. When he was on one he gave it all he had, but finished, he returned to this apartment on Harper, sometimes not leaving the place for days at a time. He had no friends, no intimates aside from Eddie Slocum. Eddie was secretary, butler, cook, chauffeur and all-around assistant to Simon Lash.

He was working around the apartment now. Lash heard him in the kitchen, then in the office in front. He heard the phone ring twice, the doorbell once, but Eddie did not come in to report. Finally, Lash heard Eddie leave the apartment and guessed that he was going out for groceries to cook dinner.

He had been gone five minutes when the doorbell rang. Lash groaned and swore softly, but did not get up from the couch. The doorbell rang again, then a voice called from the hall: "Hello, Mr. Lash?"

Lash cursed Eddie Slocum for not having locked the door on his way out. He got up and padded into the hall.

The intruder was Oscar Loomis.

"What do you want?" Lash demanded.

Loomis was taken aback. "Why, I wanted to talk to you about the Bonniwell affair. In fact, I wanted to engage your services."

"Not interested!"

Loomis exclaimed. "Not interested? I don't understand. I thought you were a regular private detective. Licensed . . ."

"I am," Lash snapped, "but I choose my cases. I'm no longer interested in the Bonniwell case."

"Yes, I understand that. Joyce — I mean, I heard you were no longer employed by Mrs. Bonniwell and you can, therefore, ethically represent another — "

"No," Lash said firmly. "I don't like the Bonniwell case."

Loomis snorted. "Look here, if it's money I'm not exactly a poor man. I'll give you a thousand dollars . . . "

"What for?"

"To represent me. That desert sheriff seems to suspect me of killing Jim Bonniwell."

"The percentage of innocent men who get executed is negligible. If you didn't kill Bonniwell they probably won't convict you."

"It's not that!" protested Loomis. "It's — well, Jim was my best friend. I want to find his murderer, bring him to justice."

"So does Rucker. Tell him the truth and he can help you as much as anyone could."

Loomis glowered "You refuse then? Even with a thousand-dollar retainer and an additional four thousand after you make the arrest?"

"Do you mind?" Lash asked. "I've got a cake in the oven and I think it's burning."

Loomis' face twisted angrily. Muttering, he turned and slammed out of the door.

Grinning crookedly, Lash went to his office and looked out to the street. The

113

olive Cadillac was parked at the curb, in front of the adjoining building.

A yellow telegram form was lying face up on Lash's desk. It was from Deacon Jones of San Francisco and read:

OSCAR LOOMIS IN JAM SIX MONTHS AGO BECAUSE WORKED THE OLD MINK GAME. CAN FURNISH PARTICULARS BUT IT WILL COST YOU ADDITIONAL FIFTY. BETTER WIRE MONEY. NEED IT BADLY.

Lash fingered the slip of paper, then shook his head and tossed it into the wastebasket beside the desk. The removal of the telegram revealed a white slip of paper on the desk, on which Eddie Slocum had scrawled:

Evelyn Price, Danceland, Figueroa Street.

Lash frowned at the sheet of paper, turned away, then reached back and scooping up the paper, stuffed it into his pocket. He went to his bedroom, undressed to shorts and went into the bathroom.

He shaved and bathed and when he came out, got a dark-blue suit from a closet. He took a tan shirt from a chiffonier drawer, added a red necktie and dressed quickly. When he finished the odor of frying steak was wafted into the bedroom.

He went into the kitchen where Eddie Slocum was setting the table. "Is there any money left, Eddie?" he asked.

"Uh-huh," Eddie replied. "The landlady hasn't caught me yet."

"Fine. Have you got fifty?"

Slocum gave it to him. "I may run out and shoot a little pool myself."

"Okay, Eddie. I probably won't be in until late."

8

WHEN they finished dinner it was seven o'clock and Lash got his hat and left the apartment. Outside he walked to Sunset, then turned west to Laurel Canyon, where there was a taxi line. He went up to the first cab driver.

"D'you know a dance hall on Figueroa called Danceland?" he asked.

"I sure do, Mister, but are you sure you want to go there? It's a clip joint."

"Well, they tell me they do the clipping painlessly," Lash retorted. "If it isn't putting you out of the way too much, suppose you drive me there?"

Thirty-five minutes later, Lash paid off the taxi and turned toward the building that contained 'Danceland.' It apparently occupied the entire second floor of a double store building. Red and blue neon signs flashed and flickered, as they advertised: '100 Beautiful Hostesses.'

Lash climbed to the second floor and

surrendered his hat at a checkroom. He moved toward the dance hall entrance and was stopped by a man in uniform. "Tickets?"

Lash looked around and saw that he had missed a ticket booth. He stepped up to it. "How much?"

"One dollar for ten tickets," the cashier told him.

"I only want one ticket — "

The girl gave him a scornful look. "You've got to buy at least ten to get in. That's good for ten dances."

Lash gave her a dollar and received ten tickets. The doorman glanced at them and let him into the ballroom. Lash blinked at the strange sight.

The place was lighted by soft red and blue lights around the walls and additional blue and red spotlights played upon eight or ten couples dancing on the floor, to the accompaniment of a five-piece band.

At the back of the room, at least a hundred men were watching the dancers. They were not idle because of a lack of girls with which to dance, for there was a long line of them at the edge of the

117

dance floor, just inside a velvet railing. The girls were humming, swaying and ogling the men outside the ropes.

As Lash got his bearings the band stopped playing and most of the couples left the floor. A few men from the outside went into the enclosure, selected willing partners from the line and moved out to dance. The intermission lasted approximately thirty seconds and then the band swung into a new number.

Lash threaded his way through the crowd of men. He felt oddly warm and embarrassed. This was a new experience to him.

At least a third of the men in the crowd were sailors. One half of the others were men over forty; many of them bald.

Turning to look at the dancers, Lash was startled to see an attractive blonde smile and wink at him. He half-smiled in return and the girl signaled him with her head. He looked at the tickets in his hand, took a deep breath and headed toward the entrance of the dance floor. The blonde met him and promptly held up her arms to dance.

Instinctively Lash put one arm about

her and in sudden panic realized that he had not danced in ten years. He was given a momentary respite, however, for at that moment, the band stopped playing.

The blonde dropped her arms, smiled up at Lash and said, sweetly, "Ticket, please."

Lash held up his handful of tickets and the girl promptly took them all. "I'll tell you when they're used up," she murmured, and added instantly: "You're new here, I haven't seen you before. Do you like it? You know, I saw you the minute you came in and I knew you'd ask me to dance. I'll bet you're a swell dancer. I know I'm going to like you. A girl gets so tired of dancing with sailors and old geysers with bald heads. The old ones are the worst, they don't want to dance. They want to maul you."

All that came out in a rush and along about halfway, the band started playing again and before Lash quite realized it, he was moving stumblingly with the girl, in what might have been called dancing by an uncritical observer. The blonde was not critical, however.

She said: "Oh, you're a swell dancer. Just my height, too. I like a tall man. I hate the short, fat ones, especially the bald geezers. They're worse than the sailors, although the sailors when they just come ashore from a long cruise are pretty bad. I knew you were a gentleman, though, the minute I laid eyes on you and I said, there's a fella's going to ask me to dance. I just know it. You're new here, I haven't seen you before. Do you like me? What's your name? Mine's Betty. Are you married? I'll bet you are; all the good-looking men are married. That's what makes it so tough . . . "

It was then that Lash saw Evelyn Price. She was wearing a white evening gown with red trimming that matched her flaming hair. She was just coming out of a door marked, 'Ladies' Lounge,' but already a sailor was trying to head her off.

Lash mumbled, "Excuse me," and left the blonde standing on the dance floor.

He beat the sailor by six feet, said, "Dance?" and caught hold of her.

The sailor yelped, "Hey, you lousy! . . . " but Lash whirled the redhead away and a bouncer in a dinner jacket descended upon the sailor.

Lash had danced less than a dozen feet when the music stopped. Evelyn Price said, "Ticket," and held up her hand. That was the first time she looked at Lash's face. Her eyes widened.

"Why! . . . " she gasped.

Lash grinned frostily. "Hello, Evelyn."

"What are you doing here?" she exclaimed.

"Dancing. This is a dance hall, isn't it?"

Her nostrils flared. "It is, but where's your ticket?"

Lash winced. "Some gold-digger grabbed them all from me. I'll get some more . . . "

"You do that," Evelyn said coolly.

Lash headed for the cashier and bought another dollar's worth of tickets. By the time he returned to the dance floor, the band had struck up again and Evelyn Price was in the arms of the big sailor.

Lash gritted his teeth and joined the spectators outside the ropes. He timed the dance and discovered that it lasted less than two minutes. But the sailor stopped at the far side of the floor with Evelyn and Lash saw him give her another ticket. He wondered how many tickets the sailor had.

The blonde he had deserted caught sight of Lash and came up on the inside of the velvet rope. "Say, what was the idea?" she demanded. "Running off in the middle of a dance?"

"You got my tickets, didn't you?" Lash retorted.

"What tickets? I only got tickets for what you danced. I thought you was a gentleman . . . "

"Skip it, sister," Lash snapped.

The blonde wasn't willing to skip it, but Lash moved back in the crowd. When next he dared venture toward the railing, Evelyn was still dancing with the sailor.

She danced with him for eight more dances. Then the sailor made a beeline for the cashier, to acquire additional tickets. Lash pounced down upon her, exhibiting his tickets.

"Sorry," Evelyn said, "I've got the next dance."

"With me," Lash said firmly. "This is

how he got you away from me."

"No, it wasn't. You didn't have any tickets. You owe me one, now."

"Here're ten; let's dance."

The orchestra started up and Lash put his arm about Evelyn and shoved her out upon the dance floor. She fell in step instinctively, but exclaimed almost immediately: "You stepped on my foot, you clumsy ox."

"The blonde I danced with before didn't have any complaints about my dancing," Lash retorted.

"Then why didn't you continue with her?"

"Because I like redheads — and you have to dance with anyone who has a ticket."

"Not necessarily; if I don't like a man's dancing I can suggest sitting it out. They usually do."

"Fine," snapped Lash. "Let's sit out these tickets."

"All right, but remember — the management doesn't allow necking."

Lash grinned crookedly and walked with Evelyn Price to the cushioned benches along the far side of the dance floor, where two or three couples were already sitting.

They sat down and Lash leaned against the wall and watched the dancers. Beside him, Evelyn Price sat stiffly for a moment or two. When the current dance finished, she held out her hand. Lash put a ticket in it.

"Well?" she said then.

"It's nice here," Lash replied.

"Is that why you came?"

"Why not? I don't get out much and this seemed like an interesting place."

"You didn't know I was working here?"

"Why, how would I know?"

She started a retort, then changed her mind. Another dance finished and he gave her another ticket. He estimated that he was good for a total of twenty minutes, counting a dance as a minute and a half and, the intermissions a half minute. The question was, how long could Evelyn Price hold out?

She sat primly for six solid dances and glancing covertly at her, he saw her chin firm and her nostrils flaring in triumph. He suddenly handed her his remaining tickets.

"I'm holding my place for four dances. Don't move or I'll report you to the manager."

She gave him a startled look, but he chuckled and cut across the dance floor. At the cashier's window he put down a ten-dollar bill. "One hundred tickets," he said.

"Yes, sir!" exclaimed the cashier, beginning a swift count. When she finally handed the tickets to Lash, they made a stack two inches thick. He held the hand containing the tickets behind his back and returned to Evelyn Price.

She gave him a defiant glance. "I can stick it out as long as you can," she told him.

He sat down. "Fine, because these hundred tickets will last exactly three hours and twenty minutes . . . and my feet hurt, anyway."

She cried out in dismay when she saw the handful of tickets. "I can't stand it . . . "

"Why, you just said you could stick it out as long as I could. It's ten after nine now. These will hold me until twelve thirty."

She turned toward him. "What do you want?"

"Nothing," he said, "just your company. That's why you work here, isn't it?"

"I work here because I've got to work — and this is the only thing I know. You think it's a crummy job for a girl to have? There's worse things . . . "

"I wasn't criticizing your choice of a job," Lash said. "I wasn't criticizing anything about you. In fact — I admire you."

"What?"

"I admire you."

She looked at him sharply. "Then why are you hounding me?"

"I'm not. I came here for pleasure, not business."

She sniffed. "I'll bet!"

"How much?"

"How much what?"

"How much'll you bet?"

"Cut it out," she cried fiercely. "You know what I've gone through . . . what I'm going through. I'm having a hard enough time without your — "

"I know," he said, "I don't want to make it any harder for you. Forget it. I came here for a good time . . . "

She sighed in surrender. "All right, Mister, you win. Give me the tickets and we'll go. The boss'll let me go if I turn in ten dollars' worth of tickets."

He got up. "I didn't know that. I could have saved you a lot of trouble . . . "

"It's all right," she said, without spirit. "I've got to change my dress. Meet me outside at the foot of the stairs, in ten minutes."

He nodded and leaving her, redeemed his hat from the check room. He descended leisurely to the street. He waited two minutes, then suddenly muttered and walked to the corner, two doors away.

9

FROM there he walked to the alley and looked in. It was dark except for a single electric light bulb over a door at the third building, the rear of the dance hall.

She came aside of three minutes, running silently. When she reached the sidewalk, Lash stepped out.

"Hello," he said casually.

She cried out in consternation. "For the love of Mike, what are you?"

"A sucker. But I don't like a stand-up. Shall we take a taxi?"

She wilted. "I guess so . . . "

He led her to the corner and signaled a cruising cab. Helping her in, he climbed in beside her.

"Where to, Mister?" the cabby asked.

Lash looked inquiringly at Evelyn. "Third and Vermont," she said listlessly.

Ten minutes later, without a word having been spoken between them, he helped her out of the cab and paid the bill. She nodded to a fourth-rate hotel up the street a little ways.

"It's not as ritzy as Westwood, but it's home," she said cynically.

He walked to the door with her and in the light from the lobby he saw that her face was worried.

He shook his head and when she turned to go in he followed her. In the dingy lobby, a pasty-faced clerk looked blankly at them. They went into the automatic elevator and Evelyn pushed the button for the fourth floor.

Her room was at the rear of the corridor. When she unlocked it and opened the door, a whiff of stale air assailed Lash. She switched on the lights and Lash looked at one of the dreariest rooms he had ever seen.

She sensed his revulsion. "What do you expect for four dollars a week? I told you I was broke."

She took off her coat and threw it on a sagging bed, then sat down on the edge of the bed. She nodded to a rickety rocking chair beside the window.

"All right, now, let's get it over."

"Well," said Lash, "if it'll make you

feel better to talk, all right. But I might as well tell you at the beginning that I'm no longer working on the Bonniwell case."

"What do you mean? I read in the papers — "

"That a private detective named Lash went to Ocelot Springs with Mrs. Bonniwell? Sure, I was still working for her then. I quit on the way back."

"But why?"

"I didn't like the work."

She stared at him for a moment, her eyes drawn together. She shook her head wearily. "I'm almost out of my mind. What's it all about? Jim . . . "

"You were in love with him?"

Her eyes showed pain, but she shook her head. "No, I wasn't in love with Jim Bonniwell. I was infatuated with . . . well, not with him. It was — "

"The dance hall?" he suggested and saw her eyes brighten.

"Yes. You saw what it was like. Sailors, middle-aged men sneaking a night out . . . riffraff who couldn't or don't want to go to regular dance halls . . . Well, you can imagine what it was like when I first met Jim Bonniwell. Yes, I'll admit he was drunk when he first came there. But he came again, sober. He took me out to a night club. He bought things for me . . . and I hated the dance hall."

He nodded. "I think I can understand. You knew he was married?"

"Oh yes. I didn't care. I knew, too, that he'd walk out on me some time. I didn't care about that. I just wanted . . . what I got . . . for as long as I could get it. But that's over now and I'd like to forget it."

"Maybe they won't let you. Bonniwell was murdered, you know."

"That's what the late evening papers said. I tried to tell him once that he was playing with the wrong kind of people."

"Welker and Castlemon?"

She frowned. "I ought to keep my mouth shut."

"Don't tell me anything you don't want to tell. But if it makes you feel better to get it out of your system . . . it won't get any further."

"I don't think it makes much difference. They didn't arrest Leon Welker?"

"No. But that doesn't mean they

won't. But what makes you think it was Welker?"

"I don't know if it was, but Jim brought him up to the apartment a couple of times. I could see right away what he was. A slicker. And when I heard what the racket was . . . "

"The mink farm? I was out at the farm. They do have some minks there, not as many as I'd expected considering the money they were talking about, but they had several hundred. I'm not posted on the price of mink furs, but I understand a mink coat costs a lot of money."

"You're telling me. But — aren't you hep to the racket?"

Lash pursed up his mouth. "Well, I'm not quite sure of the exact technique, but — " He broke off in the middle of the sentence and catapulted toward the door. Jerking it open he plunged out into the hallway.

He was too late. All he caught was a glimpse of a dark-brown suit disappearing into the automatic elevator. He ran toward the elevator, but the door was closed before he got to it.

He looked around for the stairs, saw

them at the far end and swore softly. He walked back to Evelyn Price's room. She was standing, her face taut, eyes wide and nostrils flaring.

Lash looked at the floor just inside the door, then said: "Let me see it."

"See what? I don't — "

"The note that was stuck under the door."

She seemed to cringe. "There wasn't any note. I don't know — I got scared when you jumped up like that."

"Give it to me," he ordered sharply. He advanced upon her and laid his hand on one of her arms crossed over her breasts.

She reached down and brought out a soiled piece of paper. On it was printed in pencil:

KEEP YOUR MOUTH SHUT, OR ELSE.

"Who knew that you were moving to this place?" Lash asked.

She shook her head. "No one. I don't know . . . No, I didn't even give them my address at the agency. I gave them . . . the old one on

133

Wilshire. But . . . how did you find me?"

"Through the agency. I guess if they took a five-dollar bribe from me, they took it from someone else. You can't stay here."

"But where'll I go? I paid out the last of my money for this room. What I earned tonight . . . "

He reached into his pocket, brought out the few bills he had remaining and extended a twenty to her. She looked at the money and shook her head.

"No, I don't think I want to go into that . . . again!"

"This is a loan," Lash said roughly. "Get into a taxi and ride down to the Southern Pacific Depot. Go through the ladies' room and out by another door. Get another taxi and go somewhere — not to this neighborhood. Hollywood would be better for you. You can get into a bungalow court for not much more than you're paying here. Get in touch with me at my office tomorrow. Do you still have my card?"

"Yes. The address is on Harper."

"That's right. Get out of here, right

now. I want to talk to your marijuana-smoking clerk downstairs."

He turned abruptly and walked out of the room. Down in the lobby he approached the pasty-faced, blank-eyed clerk. "The man who asked for Miss Price's room a few minutes ago . . ." Lash began.

"Who?" the clerk asked stupidly.

"Miss Evelyn Price. A man asked for her room number . . ."

"Yeah, didn't you find it? It's on the fourth floor, Room — "

"*I* didn't ask for it. I came in with Miss Price. Another man asked later, a man in a brown suit . . ."

"Who was he looking for?"

Lash gritted his teeth, then turned on his heel and walked out of the lobby. A taxi was parked at the curb. He went up to it and peered in, but it was vacant, except for the driver who was reading a comic magazine.

A private car was parked in front of a residence next to the hotel, but it too was vacant. Lash walked to the corner and waited there for five minutes until he saw Evelyn Price come out of the hotel with a bag. He saw her look around, then step into the taxi.

Alert now, Lash watched the taxi pull away. No other car started up and no one came out of the shadows. Sighing in relief, Lash turned and walked a block when he found another taxi and ordered the driver to take him home.

Paying off the cab, on Harper, Lash saw that there was a light in the second-floor window. It was only a quarter to eleven. Eddie Slocum had apparently come in early or had not gone out at all.

He let himself in with the latchkey and climbed the stairs. From the office, Eddie Slocum called "Chief?"

Lash went to the office and discovered Eddie in his swivel chair with his shoes on the desk. Eddie grinned and put his feet on the floor.

"You got in early, Chief," he remarked.

"So did you."

"Oh, I didn't go out."

"Why not?"

Eddie shrugged. "Didn't feel like it."

Lash exhaled heavily. "Cut it, Eddie. I'm in no mood for games."

"Neither am I, Chief, but — how do we stand?"

"Where we always did. You've been here long enough — and through enough — to know that."

"I didn't mean that, Chief. I . . . uh, oh, I know about the . . . regular stuff. I mean, are we working, or aren't we?"

"Damn you, Eddie, I told you I got fired by Mrs. Bonniwell this afternoon."

"Uh-huh, that's what you said. Well, you wouldn't want to hear this, then."

"Do I have to choke it out of you?"

Eddie Slocum's eyes lit up. "This place has been as busy as preview night at Grauman's Chinese Theatre. First of all, there was a telegram — two telegrams, although they didn't come together."

"From Deacon Jones and the Claypool outfit? I saw those that came this afternoon and filed them in the wastebasket."

"These are new ones. Maybe I better tell you about the visitors first. There were three, all told. Fella named Oscar Loomis — the subject of our 'Frisco inquiries."

"I know the gentleman and he, too, was here previously. When you were out for the groceries."

"Okay, then you know what he wanted. Or do you? He offered a two-thousand-dollar retainer . . ."

"He's raised the ante. Who were the others?"

"Young fella claimed to be sheriff of Ocelot County. He didn't look like it."

"He is, though. Sheriff Rucker. All right, who was number three?"

"He just left ten minutes ago. You'd never guess who this one was."

"Do I *have* to guess?" Lash snapped.

"It was Vincent Springer. Yep, the president — "

"Springer?" exclaimed Lash. "How do you know it was Springer?"

"He said so. Smooth-looking, about forty-five. He seemed pretty disappointed when you weren't here, but he wouldn't wait and he didn't say he'd come back."

"Did he say what he wanted?"

"Uh-uh. He figured I was the butler. Not at all like Loomis, who gave me a sales talk — I mean to sell you. Or Sheriff

Rucker, who said he'd be back."

"Tonight?"

"Well, he said, later, and that was about two hours ago."

Lash nodded. "All right, the telegrams now."

Slocum got them out of a drawer and Lash glanced at the top one, from Deacon Jones:

WHY DON'T YOU WIRE MY HUNDRED? LANDLORD ABOUT TO EVICT ME. HAVE LOCATED VICTIM OF OSCAR LOOMIS SWINDLE. SEND MONEY AND WILL GET FULL DETAILS FOR YOU.

"Money," muttered Simon Lash, "that's all these blackmailing detectives think about." He glanced at the telegram from the Claypool agency and found it to be in a similar vein.

OSCAR LOOMIS ACCUSED SEVERAL MONTHS AGO OF SWINDLING RETIRED GROCER OF $1,000. CASE SETTLED OUT OF COURT. WILL TRY TO LOCATE SUBJECT OF SWINDLE, BUT INSIST YOU SEND RETAINER AT ONCE.

Lash tossed the telegrams back on the desk. "How do we stand financially, Eddie?"

"Not so good, Chief. I paid a couple of the small bills, but we still owe the rent. I've got about fourteen bucks left — not counting the five hundred, of course. But I have to deliver that in the morning."

Lash nodded. "Better go down to the Western Union office and wire that money to Deacon Jones and Claypool. At the same time tell the Claypool outfit they're fired. They're two hours behind Deacon, right along. Tell the Deacon to carry through . . . In the morning you'll have to sell some more books to make up the five hundred . . ."

"Huh? You're going to go through with that?"

"Not for Mrs. Bonniwell . . ."

"Grab Loomis then!" exclaimed Eddie. "A two-thousand-buck retainer would put us on Easy Street."

"I can't take Loomis . . . yet. I've got to find out where he was at nine forty-five this evening."

"What happened?"

"Nothing particular, but if he was

around Vermont and Third and wore a brown suit, we can't accept him as a client."

Eddie Slocum grunted. "You want to know what I got this afternoon?"

"Shoot."

"Well, first of all, the Price girl. The agency only had her Wilshire address, but — "

"You can skip her. I'm up to date on her."

Eddie grinned. "I thought so. Okay; Mrs. Bonniwell. You wanted a timetable on her for yesterday. Here it is." He took a slip of paper out of his pocket. "Mrs. Bonniwell, you know, lives in a swell joint out in Beverly Hills. I tried to buzz her maid, but no soap, so I had to pick it up from the neighbor's Filipino gardener. He says he saw her leave the house at ten to eight in her car and come back again around ten. Naturally, he didn't know where she'd been, but I gave him a regular third degree and he seemed to remember that she looked all fixed up when she came in, so I figured — "

"Spare me the details of your brainwork," Lash said sarcastically. "Just

141

give me the conclusion. She'd been to the beauty parlor."

"Right. I even located the place on Rodeo Drive. Check. She was there from ten minutes after eight until quarter to ten, which brought her back to her place around ten. She came out again at ten thirty and drove off again. She didn't come before noon when the Filipino quit work — he only works half days.

"Damn," said Lash. "She didn't telephone here until almost three thirty and it was a quarter to four before she got here. Practically five and a half hours that we don't know a damn thing about. She could have driven to Ocelot Springs in that time . . . "

"But not back again," said Eddie. "I looked it up on the map. It's a hundred and seventy-eight miles from here."

Lash snapped his fingers. "I didn't know how far to go back when I talked to you on the phone, Eddie. I want the night before that. And I don't just want to be told she went to bed at ten o'clock and woke up in the morning. I want to know for sure that she was in that house all night."

"Jeez, Chief, how can I get that? I told you the maid was a sourpuss and wouldn't talk."

"How sour is she?"

"Well, she's about forty and — Nix, Chief, I couldn't make love to her . . . "

"Do you want *me* to do it?"

"Well, I'll trade her for the redhead and give you something to boot."

Lash regarded Eddie coldly. "If you can't handle a simple little job like that, perhaps I can get someone from the Otis Agency, someone who lacks your fine scruples . . . "

"Oh, I'll do it," growled Eddie.

"I'll give you until noon. Now, what about Welker?"

"Well, the landlady of the Wilshire place says a fella answering his description visited there two-three times."

"What do you mean, description? I didn't give you any."

"You said he was a slicker."

"That's no description. Loomis might come into that classification. Didn't the landlady over there hear any name? Loomis visited there, too, and I want to distinguish one from the other."

"Well, I missed on that. But I got a line on Welker. He had a guest card at the Sunset Athletic Club. They remember him there because he was very lucky drawing to inside straights. And getting full houses."

Lash nodded. "He probably stole a trunkful of guest towels, too. What else?"

"Nothing more on Welker. But I talked again to the teller from the Sheridan National. Bonniwell and Springer went out a lot together and my stoolie said they had some kind of business dealings outside the bank. He's seen personal checks given by Springer to Bonniwell. For big chunks, five and ten g's."

Lash's eyes narrowed thoughtfully. "All of this is pretty thin, Eddie. It probably makes a picture but I can't see it. I wish to hell I could get one solid chunk that I could sink my teeth into. These people are all a bunch of liars, but so far I haven't been able to cram any of the big lies down their throats and make them holler. This fellow, Welker, probably could tell the whole story, but he's slippery as an eel. And he smells just about as bad as an overripe eel."

"Well," said Eddie, "if he comes up here again we might take him into a bedroom and make him talk."

"I don't approve of the rough stuff," Lash replied. "But — I'll give it some thought. I don't like the way Welker waxes his mustache."

Eddie Slocum got his hat. "I'll take the car, because I may have to run all the way down to Vine before I find a Western Union office open."

"All right, you'd better go before I change my mind. I'm not too keen on sending that money."

Eddie left the apartment and Lash seated himself in the swivel chair. He leaned back, staring at the wall across the room, as he tried to sift out the snatches of information he and Eddie Slocum had picked up since Joyce Bonniwell had first come in to persuade Lash to find her husband, suffering from amnesia,

Lash sighed. That amnesia story had held up no longer than anything else in this muddle. Lash scowled at the telephone. He was tempted to pick it up and call Joyce Bonniwell and ask her where she had spent those five and a half hours the day before. Would she tell him?

He thought about it. She'd probably tell him something, but it would probably be a lie. Lies seemed to come easier to her than truth. Joyce had come a long way these last ten years.

Lash's eyes glowed. How young and blind he had been in those days.

The doorbell rang. Lash got up and went to the stairs leading down to the door on the first floor.

"Use your key, Eddie!" he yelled.

A muffled shout answered him and the person at the door rattled the doorknob. Cursing softly, Lash ran down the stairs.

He gripped the doorknob and pulled on the door.

Lightning exploded in his face and a clap of thunder buffeted him and sent him reeling back. He tripped and fell into a black velvet cloak that shut off all light and sound.

10

THE voice was off-key and made three syllables of the word 'tumbling' as it sang over and over the phrase, "I'm drifting along with the tumbling tumbleweed." It was probably all the singer knew of the song and after listening to it eight or ten times, Simon Lash became so annoyed he burst out: "For Christ's sake get a new song!"

The song stopped and a voice said: "Ah, he's awake and as cheerful as ever!"

Lash opened his eyes, blinked and pressed his eyes shut tightly. For a moment he lay still as his senses returned. Then he tore his eyes open and looked up it the grinning face of young Sheriff Rucker of Ocelot Springs.

"Hi, neighbor," Rucker greeted him.

Lash swung his feet to the floor, sat up and saw that he was in his book-lined library. The sudden movement caused a twinge of pain in his forehead and he put up his hand. It touched a pad of adhesive tape and bandage, under which was a splitting ache.

"It's just a scratch," Rucker assured him. "But an eighth of an inch more to the left and the auctioneer would have been selling off your books to pay the funeral expenses."

"Who was it?"

"Oh, I was going to ask you that. I came along ten minutes ago, found the door downstairs open a couple of inches and you lying inside."

"Has Eddie got back yet?"

"Your assistant? Haven't seen him. You don't know then who took a shot at you?"

"No one. I bumped my head against the door."

"Come again," said Sheriff Rucker. "You've got a powder burn under that bandage. Besides, I saw the bullet in the stairs. A .38. Who did it?"

"I didn't see him. The doorbell rang and I went down to answer it. I opened the door and then lightning hit me. Maybe you did the shooting."

"Why," said Sheriff Rucker cheerfully, "I might have, at that. But right now I can't think of a reason for popping you off. Can you?"

Lash got to his feet and stood still for a moment, fighting down the nausea that threatened to overwhelm him. He moved to the office. Sheriff Rucker followed him.

The top right-hand drawer of his desk was pulled open. "Snooping?" he accused the sheriff.

"Just looking for bandages."

"In my desk?"

"Well, I found them in the bathroom, but you know, while I was looking through the desk I accidentally came across some telegrams. Who's the Deacon? And the Claypool Agency?"

Lash seated himself in the swivel chair. He was looking at the sheriff, when the doorbell downstairs rang twice, shortly, and Eddie Slocum's feet came pounding up the stairs. He broke into the office, saw the sheriff, then the bandage on Lash's face.

He bristled. "He bust you, Chief?"

Lash waved impatiently at him. "Spare

149

me the heroics. Someone took a shot at me."

"Who?"

"He didn't leave his card."

Sheriff Rucker laughed. "You kill me, Lash. Never saw a man so even-tempered. Always mad."

Lash regarded him coldly. "Cut out the hick act. You can't throw me off guard. What d'you want?"

Rucker screwed up his face. "If you're ready to play ball, I'll lay my cards on the table. You look at them and if you can fill in, let's close it up. All right?"

"The county pays you, Rucker," Lash said. "So far I've been working for nothing . . . I won't help you land your murderer until I get a paying client."

"I guess I made a mistake letting you get away from Ocelot Springs. But . . . I've been talking to your cops. I think they'd take a hand if I nudged them a little more."

"I don't scare, Rucker. If you want to talk, go ahead. If not . . . " Lash shrugged.

Rucker studied him a moment, then sighed. "I got the report from our coroner. Bonniwell was killed just a little while before the boys called me. Between eleven and twelve. How does that strike you for alibis?"

"For Mrs. Bonniwell? Perfect. She was at the beauty parlor until almost ten in the morning. She left with me for Ocelot Springs at four in the afternoon."

"I'm going to check that, Lash."

"Go ahead. I may as well tell you, though, that I'm no longer representing Mrs. Bonniwell."

Rucker looked sharply at Lash. "So? How come?"

"Ask her."

Rucker chewed his lower lip. "You're pretty interested in Oscar Loomis. Why? It would take him nine or ten hours to drive to Ocelot from 'Frisco. Say he left at nine thirty. He couldn't possibly have got to Ocelot more than an hour before he showed up. At least eight hours after Bonniwell was killed."

Lash made no comment. Rucker scowled. "All right, maybe he didn't come from 'Frisco. Maybe he left the night before and was hanging around Ocelot all day. Naturally, I'm going to

151

check all that pretty thoroughly. It takes time. What about this Vincent Springer? He walked out of his bank yesterday morning and no one's seen him since. Where does he fit into this?"

"He's the president of the Sheridan National; Bonniwell's bank."

"I know that. But why are you so interested in him?"

"I'm not. I talked to him when I was working on the amnesia angle. I haven't seen him since."

"But he was here this afternoon."

Eddie Slocum began rolling his eyes and Lash said, crisply: "Better burn your notes from now on, Eddie. Sheriff Rucker goes through desk drawers and waste-baskets."

Rucker grinned. "All right, so I saw the list of callers Slocum made. Loomis called. Springer was here, too."

"Look, Chief," Eddie Slocum cut in. "There's blood coming through the bandage. Don't you think I ought to call a doctor?"

"It's only a scratch, Eddie," said Sheriff Rucker. "And I fixed it up okay. I was going to be a doctor before the folks elected me sheriff."

"You'd a made a good doctor," Eddie said, emphasizing the last word.

Rucker ignored the dig. He went on: "I've been doing a little work since I got to town. I located the love nest on Wilshire, but the canary's flown."

"She moved to a hotel," said Lash. "The Brooker, near Third and Vermont."

"Your generosity overwhelms me," Rucker said sarcastically. "I won't waste my time going there. She's skipped again . . . otherwise you wouldn't be giving me the address. Thanks just the same."

"I'm swapping you that information for some you may have picked up," Lash said. "The blonde who registered with Bonniwell at the Ocelot Springs Hotel."

"Oh, I'll tell you about her. She got a flat tire at Mojave. The garage man who fixed it remembered the license number. I checked it with the State Motor vehicle Department. The car's Bonniwell's — a Buick coupé. But where it is now, I don't know."

"If you've got such a drag with the Los Angeles police," Lash asked, "why not put it on the air?"

"I did. And they did. No results yet . . . So you won't talk?"

"I've got a headache," said Lash. "And it's late and I think I'll go to sleep. The Ocelot Springs Hotel stuffs its beds with cobblestones. Tell them that, will you?"

"I will . . . when I get back. Well, see you later."

"I hope not," Lash said disagreeably, as Rucker went out.

After Eddie Slocum had made sure the sheriff had gone, he padded into the office. "Who did it, Chief?"

"I told the truth. I didn't see his face. I thought it was you ringing the doorbell."

"Uh-uh, I had to run all the way down to Vine Street."

"Well, I guess it doesn't make any difference. Unless . . . one of the other visitors has a brown suit. How about it?"

"Loomis? No, dark-blue. Springer . . . mm. He was wearing a raincoat, but I'm pretty sure he had a gray suit underneath."

"Which doesn't prove anything. In the time he had he could have changed his suit. You know, Eddie, the more I think of this Loomis the more I dislike him. He's got too much money. I'd like to know where he got it."

"Deacon Jones gave you a lead on that. He's a con man."

"Mm. The Deacon says he swindled *one* customer — and he probably made restitution there to keep from going to jail. That doesn't mean, however, that he hasn't worked his game on others. A lot of people hate to squawk when they get skinned. Makes them out chumps. I think I'll give Mr. Loomis some attention tomorrow and see if I can't separate him from some of his money."

"Why not tonight?"

"Uh-uh. I'd spend half the night trying to locate him. And I'm too tired."

11

THE odor of frying bacon awakened Simon Lash the next morning. He bounced out of bed, headed for the bathroom and had showered and donned most of his clothing when Eddie Slocum yelled into the bedroom.

"Breakfast is ready, Chief!"

Lash went into the kitchen and seated himself at the table. He drank his orange juice, put sugar and cream into his coffee and stabbed at a piece of bacon. Then he noticed the morning paper beside his plate, opened to page six.

Lash fold the item quickly. The headlines over it read:

MURDER VICTIM'S CAR FOUND

Police Seek Girl

The three-paragraph story told of the finding of Buick coupé on a side street in Barstow, registered in the name of James Bonniwell, N. Rodeo Drive, Beverly Hills. The car had been the object of a statewide search on behalf of the police, since the driver, a young woman, was wanted for questioning in the murder of James Bonniwell, at Ocelot Springs. According to the report made by the sheriff of Ocelot Springs, a woman had arrived at the desert town with James Bonniwell, the evening before his death. She had registered at the Ocelot Springs Hotel as Mrs. Bonniwell, but had remained in her room only a few minutes, after which she had got into the car and disappeared.

After reading the item, Simon Lash tapped it with his finger. "Eddie," he said, "we haven't been paying enough attention to this woman."

"I never heard about her until last night. That was the first I knew Bonniwell had dragged a dame out to the desert with him."

Lash scowled. "This Bonniwell played a large field. And he liked variety. His wife's a brunette, the Price girl is a decided redhead and they say this one's a platinum blonde."

"He liked blondes before," Slocum said. "Remember what I got from the bank teller? About Bonniwell and his boss, Springer, being at the Troc with a pair of blondes?"

"I remember that," Lash admitted. "And I think this blonde could tell us a lot of things we want to know, since she was in his confidence enough to be taken out to the mink ranch. After breakfast you'd better try to find her."

"How? The whole police force is looking for her now."

"They're not as smart as you are," Lash said, grinning crookedly. "And they don't play pool with one of Springer's bank tellers."

"Yeah, but Peabody — that's the teller — won't be shooting pool during the day. I can't go up to the bank because he'd be scared stiff if I told him I was a detective."

"Well, I'll leave the *modus operandi* up to you. But I want to find that girl and I want to find her before the cops do. He must have had another love nest somewhere."

"He had more nests than a traveling

sea gull," Eddie Slocum snorted.

Lash nodded. "I'll carry through on Loomis today. We need a client badly and he looks like our best bet, since he's got the money."

"Suppose he turns out to be it?"

"Then we get only the retainer. I'll see that it's a stiff one."

Finished with his breakfast, Lash got his hat and left the apartment. Outside he debated for a moment between taking the coupé out of the garage and hiring a taxi. He finally decided on the taxi and walked down to Sunset Boulevard.

Ten minutes later he entered the Sunset Athletic Club. The clerk at the desk saw him and promptly put on his mask.

"Good morning, Mr. Lash."

"Hello, Charles," Lash replied. "Is Mr. Oscar Loomis staying here at the club?"

"I don't know, Mr. Lash."

"Well, look on your register."

The clerk made no move to consult his records Lash gave him a sharp glance. "Oh, the hush is on, eh?"

"I'm sorry, we're not permitted to give out information about the guests."

159

"Fine," said Lash, "then trot out Paul Plennert."

"I'm sorry, but Mr. Plennert is tied up at the moment."

Lash bared his teeth. "Tied up, huh? All right, I'll tie him up — in knots."

He strode quickly around the desk and headed for the door of the club manager's office. The clerk moved from his desk and blocked the door.

"You can't go in, Mr. Lash," he said, his face whitening. "Mr. Plennert left orders."

"Step aside," Lash said in a loud tone.

The clerk winced and shot a glance about the lobby. A white-haired, pink-cheeked man was watching the scene, his mouth slightly agape.

"Please, Mr. Lash," the clerk pleaded. "Don't create a scene. The members — "

"Are a bunch of stuffed shirts," Lash yelled. "And the biggest stuffed shirt in this goddam joint is Paul Plennert . . . "

The door behind the clerk was jerked open and the angry face of Plennert showed over the clerk's shoulder. "Mr. Lash," he said severely. "What is the meaning of this?"

"What's the idea of the brush-off, Plennert?" Lash demanded. "I want to talk to you. Not next week, or tomorrow, but now."

"I have nothing to discuss with you, Lash," Plennert retorted. "And if you create a disturbance I'll call the police."

"Call the police!" Lash cried. "Maybe they'll take you down to headquarters, along with me. Maybe they'll give you a third degree so you'll tell what you know about the murder of Jim Bonniwell . . . "

Plennert caught Lash's arm. "Come in!" he cried, in consternation. "The members . . . "

Lash followed him into the office, kicking the door shut behind them. Plennert whirled on him furiously. "Have you gone mad, Lash? Creating a scene like that out in the lobby . . . "

"I can get a lot madder, Plennert," Lash said angrily. "You try anything like that on me again and I'll create such a ruckus the police will come . . . and think how that will look in the papers? 'Police Raid Sunset Athletic Club.'"

Paul Plennert shivered. "For Heaven's

161

sake, Lash, will you let me — and the club — alone? I told you all I knew about Jim Bonniwell the other day."

"For a plain disappearance, yes. But not for murder. I need more information. We'll start with this Leon Welker that Bonniwell brought in here on a guest card."

"I don't know Welker," Plennert said, but his rolling eyes belied his statement.

Lash said impatiently, "Don't make me choke every word out of you, Plennert. You know Leon Welker, all right. He's stayed here more than once and the members have commented pretty freely on his ability to draw to inside straights."

Plennert shuddered. "Oh, *him*! I refused him admission the last time he showed up. He was a cardsharper."

"But Bonniwell sponsored him. What'd he have to say about Welker?"

Plennert's eyes clouded. "Why, uh, I didn't speak to him about the matter."

"Because Bonniwell's bank holds a mortgage on this dump?"

"That had nothing to do with it."

162

"The hell it didn't. Bonniwell and Vincent Springer between them made you jump every time they cracked the whip. Isn't that so?"

Plennert's eyes glinted. "Since you know everything, why bother to question me, Lash?"

"Because I like to see you squirm, that's why. What about Oscar Loomis?"

"I never heard of him."

"Then you'll have no objections if I ask Charlie, the clerk, if *he* ever heard of him?"

Plennert opened his mouth to protest at such high-handedness, but let the words remain unspoken as the door behind Lash was suddenly kicked in.

The white-haired, pink-cheeked club member, who had watched the tableau outside, strode in.

"Mr. Lash," he said. "I heard what you said outside this door a minute ago. About that scoundrel, Jim Bonniwell. I have some information that will interest you . . . "

"Colonel Fedderson!" cried Paul Plennert. "Please . . . the club! . . . "

Colonel Fedderson fixed Plennert with

163

a glare. "The club be damned. That thief, Bonniwell, swindled me out of five thousand dollars and I've been quiet long enough . . . "

"Please, Colonel Fedderson," pleaded Paul Plennert.

"Please, hell!" snapped the white-haired colonel. "Five thousand dollars may be cigarette money to some of these film producers you have around here, but to me, it represents the savings of thirty years of military service . . . and I'll be damned if I let it go without a complaint." He glared again at Plennert then turned to Simon Lash.

"You, sir, are investigating that thief, Bonniwell, aren't you?"

"I am, Colonel. About this money Bonniwell swindled from you? . . . "

"It was a smooth scheme and I fell for it. This man here — " he shot a baleful glance at Plennert — "was a party to it."

"I was not!" Plennert cried. "I was as much a victim as you were."

"Did you lose five thousand of your own money? You did not. You *made* money. You showed me that check from Bonniwell. That, more than Bonniwell's sales talk, got me to risk my money."

"Whoa, Colonel," Lash exclaimed. "Let's start at the beginning. What was this investment scheme? Did it by any chance have to do with minks?"

"Minks!" roared the Colonel. "Damn the slimy creatures. Yes! Bonniwell could take a sheet of paper and a pencil and prove to you that raising minks was more profitable than making gold from tin cans."

"And where were you going to raise these minks, Colonel?" Lash asked sarcastically "In your bedroom upstairs?"

"No! That's how he got me. I wasn't to have anything to do with the stinking animals. They were going to raise them. All I had to do was deposit the checks they were going to send me. Oh, he made it sound good. A mink breeds three times a year, he says, and the litters average from eight to twelve young. You sell the skins of the surplus males every six months and breed the females. At the end of a year you have two hundred or four hundred females. At the end of two years, sixteen thousand . . . "

"For Christ's sake!" Lash gasped. "You mean to tell me you fell for something like that?"

"What the hell did I know about it?" the colonel snapped. "I'm a retired infantry officer. All I know is that the general's wife wore a mink coat and the latrine rumors were that it cost two thousand dollars."

"Some even cost more," Lash said, thinking about Joyce Bonniwell's coat. "But go on, Colonel. You fell for this fairy tale . . . "

"Not right away. Not until this man, Plennert, started flashing his 'mink-profit check' around the club. I have reason to believe that Plennert was a confederate of Bonniwell's — "

"Colonel Fedderson!" screamed Plennert. "You have no right to say such a thing. That's — that's slander. I'll take it up with the board of directors . . . "

"You do that, Plennert," Colonel Fedderson said coolly. "I've already decided to appear before the board myself and prefer those charges against you . . . "

"He's got you there, Paul," Lash said, turning upon the frightened club manager. "Better come clean. Why'd Bonniwell give you that check? To shill for him? . . . "

"No. I — I bought some minks from him, yes. The check represented legitimate profit."

"Start again, Plennert," Lash cut in. "Just how much money did you invest in those minks? Actual coin of the realm. And I'll warn you beforehand — that I had a look at the books out on the Castlemon Mink Farm, at Ocelot Springs . . . "

Paul Plennert was already perspiring freely. "I don't have to answer your questions. You're not a policeman . . . "

"Oh," said Lash, "would you rather talk to a cop? Fine . . . " He reached for the phone on Plennert's desk, said, "Give me the police department . . . "

Plennert rushed to the desk and grabbed the phone out of Lash's hand. "Don't!" he cried, slamming the phone back on the hook. "I'll tell you — what I know. Bonniwell gave me the minks. I mean — " he shot a frantic look

167

at the angry Colonel Fedderson — "I mean I'd done him some favors and he gave me the certificates, showing that I owned two trios of mink. I — I didn't take it seriously until a few months later, when he gave me that check — "

"A check for twelve hundred dollars," Colonel Fedderson declared. "Supposed to represent the profit on a five-hundred-dollar investment."

"Only Plennert didn't actually put up the five hundred," Lash finished. He shook his head grimly. "A very neat racket; Bonniwell knew that Plennert would blab to everyone who listened, about his business 'investment' and those same listeners would be ready for plucking by the mastermind, Jim Bonniwell . . . "

Colonel Fedderson cleared his throat noisily. "Oh, I wasn't the only one who fell for it. There's at least a half dozen more in this club — only they won't admit it, for fear of being ridiculed."

"The old mink game," Lash murmured. "I didn't think people fell for it any more. By the way, Colonel, what did

Bonniwell tell you when your own batch of minks failed to produce the expected profit?"

Fedderson growled. "Oh, he gave me a lot of poppycock, about disease having ravaged the herd. Why — the damn scoundrel even tried to nick me for veterinarian's fees. I told him where to go. That was just before he disappeared and if you ask me, someone who was swindled by him did for him . . ."

"That would make you one of the suspects, Colonel."

"One of many. And I'll be glad to testify on behalf of the murderer. I'll even contribute to his defense fund."

"That may not be necessary, Colonel. Anyway, we've got to find him first. Now, I wonder if you could tell me one thing more. Did you ever have reason to suspect that Bonniwell had a partner in his — his enterprise? Say, another fellow club member. Perhaps . . . Vincent Springer?"

"No, no!" howled Paul Plennert. "Mr. Springer had nothing to do with the mink farm. Nothing at all."

"You're pretty vehement in your denial,

Mr. Plennert. What would *you* say, Colonel?"

Colonel Fedderson shook his head. "No, I don't think so. Bonniwell was the only one who worked on me. And — this man, here."

"I wasn't an accomplice," denied Paul Plennert. "I can prove it . . ."

"You'll have your chance, at the board of directors' meeting, tomorrow."

Simon Lash chuckled. He had never seen a man as deflated as was Plennert. He said, "Maybe you'd be a little more co-operative now, Plennert? In the matter of Bonniwell's lady friends? What do you know about a certain platinum blonde?"

"Nothing!" blustered Plennert. "I've said my last word."

"Maybe yes, maybe no. Well — thanks for everything. Especially you, Colonel."

"No thanks to me. It's time Bonniwell's character was brought out into the open. I hope you make use of the information, Lash. I've heard about your detective work and . . ."

Lash left the office, in the middle of the Colonel's laudatory commentary. On the sidewalk he stood for a moment, rubbing his chin and looking down toward Vine Street. Finally, however, he crossed the street and signaled to a westbound taxicab.

"Rodeo Drive, Beverly Hills," he told the cabby.

12

FIFTEEN minutes later the taxi stopped before the sprawling California-style house on Rodeo Drive, a street of expensive homes. Lash paid the meter charge and walked to the front door of the house.

He rang the doorbell and blinked when the apparition answered the door. No wonder Eddie Slocum had balked at 'making love' to Joyce Bonniwell's maid. The woman was enough to frighten a sex maniac.

Lash said: "I'd like to see Mrs. Bonniwell."

"'Bout what?" the woman demanded suspiciously. "We ain't buyin' any vacuum cleaners or silk stockings."

"I'm selling beauty creams, which wouldn't interest you!" Lash snarled. "Now, will you tell Mrs. Bonniwell that Simon Lash is here?"

Giving him a black look, the clock-stopper went away. Joyce Bonniwell came to the door, exclaiming. "Simon! . . . I've been telephoning you for the last hour. Come in!"

He followed her into the cool, luxuriously furnished living room. "I stopped in to tell you that I was returning your fee," he said stiffly.

"Will you stop that nonsense?" Joyce cried. "I went back looking for you on the road. I spent two hours trying to find you, before I realized that you must have taken that bus. I'm sorry . . . "

"What's up, now?" Lash asked.

She closed her eyes in a long blink and shuddered. "Sheriff Rucker just telephoned. He says that man Castlemon — the mink raiser — was murdered last night!"

Lash looked at her steadily for a moment. "From where did Rucker telephone?"

"Here in the city. His office had communicated with him. He's on his way home, now. Simon what do you think?"

He shook his head slowly. "Castlemon was my ace in the hole. I was saving him for the showdown. He knew . . . he was the only one who could have known."

"What, Simon? I don't understand . . . "

"No one else seemed to, either. But it was right there yelling at us. Castlemon *had* to know. Think back. Who was at the farm when Bon — when it happened? Welker and Castlemon. Welker said he'd run down to the village. Castlemon didn't deny that. That left Castlemon alone at the ranch — except for Bonniwell."

"I know," cried Joyce Bonniwell. "But he said he didn't hear the shot."

"That's it! You saw the farm, didn't you? How far were the mink pens from the house? A hundred feet, not more than a hundred and fifty. Did you ever hear a shotgun go off?"

"Yes, of course. But . . . " Bewilderment came to Joyce's face.

Lash nodded. "The mink pens all have open fronts. You couldn't get into one and lock yourself in soundly enough not to hear a shotgun go off in the house, a hundred feet away . . . not even if the person who fired the shotgun had all the doors and windows closed. Besides . . . there were two shots. So . . . Castlemon must have known that

Bonniwell was dead before Welker came back. He must have seen the person who did it."

"But then why didn't he speak?"

"Because the mink business was played out. Because Castlemon intended to blackmail the man who — "

"Welker? He couldn't have killed Castlemon. He's here in the city."

"Is he? You mean he was here yesterday. He could have driven out to Ocelot Springs in three and a half hours — and back again, before this morning. A check up on his alibi is in order . . . and so is one for Oscar Loomis."

"Not Oscar!" cried Joyce. "He — he was here until midnight."

"And have you seen him since? He could have been out there by dawn. As yet, we don't know just when Castlemon was killed."

"But you're wrong. You can't suspect Oscar Loomis. He was Jim's best friend. They were roommates back in college."

"I was told that before. You have told me a lot of things about Jim Bonniwell. Some of them were . . . lies."

She flinched. "You're never gentle with words, Simon."

"There's nothing gentle about murder."

"What? What are you insinuating?"

"I'm not insinuating anything. You hired me as a detective. You gave me orders to spare no one. That included yourself . . . "

"Stop it, Simon!" she gasped. "You're going too far again."

His eyes smoldered. "For the last time, Joyce, do you want me to find the murderer of Jim Bonniwell?"

"Of course, but — but you're insane to think that I . . ."

"I never said you. I said you held things back, lied to me. Why, I don't know. But I can't work unless I learn the truth. And you haven't been telling it to me. Why . . . what are you afraid of?"

She stared at him miserably. "You like to see me squirm, don't you, Simon? You never forgave me . . . "

"I had nothing to forgive," he said curtly. "And as for making you squirm, what have you got to conceal? Things about Jim Bonniwell? Hell, I know twice as much about him already as you think

I do. He was no good."

She sighed in surrender. "I shouldn't say it now. I didn't want to admit it before . . . my pride was all I had left . . . but I was going to divorce him. I would have divorced him long ago, but . . . "

"But you didn't want to admit failure? I suppose you knew about the redhead on Wilshire — and the platinum blonde?"

Her eyes widened. "What platinum blonde?"

"The one who registered with him at Ocelot Springs. Didn't you read the morning paper? She abandoned Bonniwell's Buick in Barstow."

"Platinum blonde," whispered Joyce Bonniwell.

Lash's mouth formed an O. "You know her?"

Tears were threatening. She started to nod, then shook her head. "No, I don't."

"What's her name?"

"I don't know her."

"You do. You started to admit it. She's important to this."

Her beautiful features twisted in agony.

"But it can't be. It's ridiculous . . . "

"Who is she?"

"She can't be the one I know. That — that's Vincent Springer's fiancée, Drusilla Denham."

"And she's a platinum blonde?" Lash cried.

"Yes, but — but I saw Drusilla only the other day."

"When? Before Bonniwell? . . . "

"Yes, it was last week. I stopped in to talk to Vincent about Jim and — she was there."

"You know where she lives?"

"Of course. Here in Beverly Hills."

"Then call her. Call her right now."

"But what'll I say to her?"

"Nothing particular. Invite her to tea — anything. I just want to know if she's home."

Joyce crossed the room to the telephone. She dialed a number and after a moment, said: "Emily, this is Mrs. Bonniwell. Will you tell Miss Denham I'd like to talk to her. What? . . . No, there's no message. Good-bye." She hung up and turned to Lash, her eyes wide.

"She isn't home. Hasn't been home for

178

two days. Emily, her maid, said she'd gone to Palm Springs."

"And Vincent Springer's in Palm Springs! At least he hasn't been at his bank in two days. No . . . he called at my apartment last night, when I was out. He may be back today. Call the bank, will you? Just find out if Springer's back."

She did as he requested. The result was negative. They hadn't seen Mr. Springer at the bank in two days. They didn't know where he was.

Joyce Bonniwell dropped into a chair. There was an expression of fright bordering on horror upon her face.

"It's . . . fantastic," she whispered. "Not Vincent . . ."

"Why not? This thing has as many angles as a futuristic painting. For example, did you know that Bonniwell received large sums of money from Vincent Springer? Five and ten thousand at a crack?"

"Nothing would surprise me now. Nothing, after what I've learned these past two days." Her voice sounded dull, dead.

"Then do you see why I've got to

179

know the truth? All the truth. A bit of information in itself may not seem important. But fitted into the pattern it may be the key to the whole thing. That's why I've got to have everything."

"All right, what do you want to know?"

"First of all, your relations with Bonniwell. You've admitted they weren't good — but just how bad were they?"

"Very bad. He — didn't average two weeks in a month here. That's been going on about a year. Since he had the amnesia — "

"Wait!" Lash cried. "You're not going to stick to that amnesia story?"

"But I am. I mean — I doubted it myself — but Jim stuck to it. He actually was found wandering the streets in Santa Monica. And again in Phoenix. He — he did have his name put on his clothes, just like I told you, in case he had another attack."

Lash scowled in unbelief. "And you hired the Otis Agency to shadow him?"

"Yes. But — I mean, I didn't hire them for that reason altogether. I wanted to make sure and I thought — well, I wanted evidence for the divorce."

"That's more like it," grunted Lash. "You knew about his women?"

She shuddered. "Not definitely. I mean, there was powder on his clothes sometimes, odors of perfumes that I didn't use myself. But I never dreamed about Drusilla. Why, she and Vincent were going to be married."

"That was quite a condescension on Springer's part, eh? From what I've heard about this Springer, he had a lot in common with Jim Bonniwell. Except that he was a little on the sanctimonious side. Although I admit I didn't know Bonniwell. He might have been that way, himself."

"No, Jim didn't make that much effort."

"Mm. Tell me more about Drusilla Denham. How come she's living here in Beverly Hills — alone?"

"Why," said Joyce, her eyes clouding. "I never questioned that part of it. I mean, Drusilla seemed to have money."

"Has she ever been married?"

"Not that she ever admitted. But we haven't been the closest of friends. We were thrown together more or less

181

through Jim and Vincent."

"How old is she?"

"How old is a woman? Vincent was about Jim's age, but Drusilla must have been considerably younger."

"Your own age, perhaps?"

Joyce winced. "About that. If anything, younger."

"Let's see," Lash said bluntly, "that would make her about thirty-one or two."

"I'm only thirty . . . well, thirty-one."

Lash let that pass. He knew how old she was — how old she had been ten years ago. He said: "On those occasions when you and the others made a party, did Bonniwell pay any attention to this Drusilla?"

"Not that I noticed. But as I said, Jim was away a lot during the past year. He might have — "

"All right," said Lash. "Now, tell me about Bonniwell's financial condition. You said he was broke. Did you really mean broke, or merely down to his last fifty thousand? Some people talk like that."

"I didn't mean fifty thousand," Joyce

replied. "I doubt if he had a thousand dollars. He — borrowed money from me."

"I didn't know you had any."

Her sharp white teeth bit her lower lip. "Jim gave it to me — years ago. But he got it all back. I've less than a thousand in the bank now and wouldn't have that if he'd known about it. It's — not in the Sheridan National."

"What was his salary at the bank?"

"I don't know. Perhaps twenty thousand a year."

"Umm. He cut a pretty wide path. He took in a lot of money this past year on the side and he seems to have gone through it all."

Lash drew a deep breath. "Now, what about his insurance? You said before that he had a hundred thousand dollars' worth."

Her nostrils flared a trifle. "That's right. It's still made out to me." She hesitated. "As a matter of fact, I've put in the claim. I'll need — "

"Yes, I know. I just wanted to know. Uh . . . what about the funeral?"

"Why, the body was released. It's

being shipped direct to the crematory. Today."

Lash looked at her oddly. "No funeral?"

"I couldn't stand it. Besides, Jim always said — " She stopped. "What else do you want to know? I've told you everything now."

"I guess you have." Lash nodded and moved toward the door. Then he turned. "By the way, were you at home Tuesday night?"

She stared at him in astonishment. "Tuesday night? why, that's — "

"That's right. That was the night. Where were you?"

"Here!" she cried. "And I can prove it. And that goes for last night, too. You can ask — "

" — Your maid. Eddie Slocum asked her the other day. She slammed the door in his face. Well, goodbye!"

13

HE ducked out of the house and walked to Santa Monica Avenue before he could get a cab. It was a few minutes after eleven when he tried the door of his apartment and found it unlatched.

Eddie called to him from the office. "Company, Chief!"

Lash climbed the stairs. The first person he saw was Evelyn Price. Then two large, heavy-set men sprawled over the furniture.

"Where you been, Lash?" one of them said surlily. "We been waitin' an hour for you. I'm Lieutenant Hayden and this is Sergeant Whipple."

Lash looked sourly from one to the other, then turned to Evelyn Price. She was sitting in one of the red-leather chairs, but she was ill at ease.

"She won't talk," Lieutenant Hayden said, "but I'll bet a cookie she's the little lady from the Wilshire love nest — "

185

"That's enough of that!" Lash snapped.

Hayden got lumberingly to his feet. "O–ho! So you're going to act like that, huh? All right, we'll just run you down to the station."

"Where's your warrant?"

The lieutenant took it from his pocket. "Thought we didn't have one, huh? Well, look at it, Mister Simon Lash. What do you think of it?"

"Serve it," snarled Lash. "Serve it and then stand by for the false-arrest suit. You haven't got a thing on me. I'm a licensed private detective. I haven't done a thing for which you can arrest me."

"Well, that remains to be seen," said Lieutenant Hayden, a bit less truculent. "I wasn't meanin' to serve this warrant, unless you refused to talk."

"I haven't got anything to talk about."

"Yes, you have. It's about that affair up in Ocelot Springs. We're co-operatin' with the sheriff of Ocelot County. He's asked us to question you about what happened there last night."

"Whoa," said Lash. "Rucker didn't know about that until this morning. He was still here in town at eight o'clock."

186

"Sure, but he took an airplane back. He telephoned us. We been here almost an hour."

Lash looked at Eddie Slocum for confirmation. Eddie nodded. "Miss Price had just got here, when they bust in."

Lieutenant Hayden grinned. "How about answerin' the questions, now? Where were you last night?"

"Right here. Sheriff Rucker knows that. He didn't leave until almost midnight."

"Uh-huh, he told us that. But what about from midnight to seven this morning?"

"In my bed. I didn't even get up to go to the bathroom."

"How can you prove you didn't leave the house?"

Lash jerked his head toward Slocum.

"He's no good. He works for you. We happen to know that you were up at Ocelot."

"What?"

"Uh-huh, Rucker's got proof."

Lash went to his desk and scooped up the telephone. "I want long distance," he barked into the mouthpiece, then after a moment, "Ocelot Springs, California.

Sheriff Clarence Rucker."

The call was put through inside of a minute. Sheriff Rucker's voice said: "Rucker talking. Who's this?"

"Simon Lash. Listen, Rucker, a couple of the local flat-feet are annoying me. They claim you told them that I was in Ocelot Springs last night . . . "

"That's right. I've got the proof right here."

"What proof?"

Sheriff Rucker cleared his throat. "Come up here and I'll show you."

"Do you take me for a fool, Rucker? You haven't got a thing on me and you know it. And what's more, you try any funny stuff and I'll fight extradition. It'll be two weeks before you get me up there. And what'll that do to your case?"

"It'll shoot it full of holes, Lash. I admit that. But there are things you've got to tell me."

"There's nothing I *could* tell you. Your common sense should have told you the other day that Castlemon knew who killed Bonniwell. He couldn't have helped but hear those shotgun blasts . . . unless he was deaf."

"He wasn't deaf. And Lash — I hadn't overlooked that. I wasn't ready to put the pressure on him, then. I had another angle that I wanted to clear up first. This throws it into the fire."

"That's too damn bad," Lash said sarcastically. "But it's got nothing to do with me."

"Yes, it has, Lash . . . All right, I'll tell you what I have. Remember last night when I looked over those telegrams in your office? Well, there was one of them lying near the body of Ben Castlemon."

"You're crazy, Rucker! No one came into this house after you left last night. You must have taken the telegram yourself."

"I didn't. Umm, as a matter of fact, it wasn't one of those that I'd read. It was an earlier one from Deacon Jones. It was crumpled up in a ball . . . as if it had accidentally fallen out of a pocket."

"Accidentally, or purposely."

"Well, I thought of that, too. But I couldn't figure out how anyone could have got it."

"Don't be a sap. Remember, someone tapped me on the head last night . . . "

Rucker groaned. "I was afraid you were going to pull that one."

"Well, what's the matter with it?"

"Nothing . . . from your viewpoint. But it doesn't get me anywhere."

"That's too damn bad, Rucker. Look here, you call off these local yokels and I'll swap you something. I'll give you the name of the platinum blonde."

Rucker inhaled sharply. "You know that? How? . . . "

"Never mind how I found out. You'll get on the right track once you know her name. I'll even go further and tell you the tie-up. Is it a deal?"

"I can't make a deal like that," protested Rucker. "If you know that much, you know more."

"I do — but you can't make me talk. I've got a client and the law says you can't make a private detective reveal a client's confidence."

Rucker was silent a moment. Then, "All right, Lash. I'll swap. What's her name?"

Lash gestured to Lieutenant Hayden. "Sheriff Rucker of Ocelot County wants to talk to you."

The big detective took the phone from Lash's hands. "Hello, Sheriff. This is Lieutenant Hayden of the Los Angeles Police. I've got that warrant. Huh? Okay, if you say so. It's not in our jurisdiction anyway. We was just doing you a favor. Sure, sure s'long!"

He handed the phone back to Lash, then took out the warrant and ripped it in two. "Okay, Lash. So long . . . "

Lash waited until the policemen had lumbered out, followed by Eddie Slocum. Then he said into the telephone. "The name is Drusilla Denham, Rucker. And . . . she's Vincent Springer's fiancée . . . " He chuckled and slipped the receiver onto the hook.

Eddie Slocum looked at Lash with his head cocked to one side. "Where'd you get that, Chief?"

Lash ignored him. He said to Evelyn Price: "You started to tell me something last night, when that note was slipped under the door. What was it?"

Her eyes clouded. "We were talking about Jim Bonniwell. His racket — "

"I know about that now. It would have been news last night. Bonniwell

191

was working the old mink game."

She got up. "Then there isn't anything more that I can tell you."

"Oh, but there is! Tell me about Oscar Loomis — and Leon Welker."

She exclaimed. "What? I don't — "

"Yes, you do. Your landlady on Wilshire said they'd visited there with Bonniwell."

"Jim only brought one man up to the apartment in all the time we lived there. It was — it wasn't either of those you mentioned."

"Who was it, then?"

She didn't want to tell, but finally did. "His boss, Mr. Springer."

Lash shot a quick glance at Eddie Slocum. The latter shrugged.

Lash snapped. "Well, has he got back?"

"Who? Springer? He wasn't at the bank, but — "

"But what?"

"Why, he was here last night. You remember I told you . . . "

"You said a man who gave his name as Springer was here."

"That's right."

"How do you know it was Springer? You never saw him any other time, did you?"

Eddie Slocum's mouth fell open. "Cripes!"

"It could have been Leon Welker just as well, couldn't it? You never saw *him* before. Or Loomis for that matter. They gave you names and you accepted them. To a woman like that landlady on Wilshire, Springer would have looked as much like a slicker as Welker. And he's about the same age — even if they don't look at all alike. You want to pay more attention to your descriptions, Eddie!"

A puzzled look came over Eddie's face. "I don't get the angle. What's so important which one it was?"

"The importance is that Vincent Springer walked out of his bank the other morning right after I talked to him. He hasn't been seen — for sure — since . . . And all the fingers are pointing to him right now."

"Springer! Jeez . . . I never thought . . . "

"I know you didn't!" Lash snapped. He whirled on Evelyn Price. "What did

Bonniwell think of Springer, toward the end?"

She was breathing heavily. "Why . . . why, I don't think they were such good friends any more. Since you mention it now . . . "

"Did you ever meet this Drusilla Denham?"

"Yes, but you're wrong. Jim didn't . . . "

"Still defending him, eh? Jim Bonniwell was a louse, a plain unadulterated louse. He mistreated his wife, double-crossed every friend he ever had. He even cheated on his mistress . . . "

Color flamed into her cheeks, almost matching her hair.

"I wasn't complaining, was I?" she snapped at Lash. "I was getting along fine until you butted in and messed up things. You couldn't let me alone, could you? You had to stick your nose into everything and what's it got you? Nothing but a headache, and me — it's lost me everything. Mr. Lash, I think you're a goddam son of a bitch!"

And with that she walked out of the apartment. Lash waited until he heard the door slam downstairs, then he snapped at Eddie Slocum.

"After her, Eddie! I want her new address. If you lose her, I'll bat your ears down. Get! . . . "

Eddie Slocum ducked out.

Lash went to his swivel chair, dropped in it and put his feet up on the desk. He clasped his hands behind his head and stared sightlessly at the ceiling.

The Bonniwell case had started out as a simple matter of finding a needle in a haystack. Now the haystack had been scattered over an entire ten-acre field.

14

EDDIE SLOCUM returned to the apartment two hours later. He failed to find Lash in the office and went to the library. Lash was sprawled on the leather couch, his coat thrown over a chair, shoes scattered on the floor. He was reading a green-bound book.

Slocum groaned. "Again!"

"What did you say, Eddie?" Lash asked, without taking his eyes from the book.

"I said I followed her to a tourist court on Ventura Boulevard, in North Hollywood."

"Oh," said Lash. He was silent for a moment, then, "Do you know, Eddie, the thing that always surprises me about these old Western writers is their phonetic spelling of proper names. You take this book, *Dodge City, the Cowboy Capital.* It was written by Robert Wright, one of the founders of Dodge City. He was also the first mayor and one of the men who hired Wyatt Earp as a marshal. You'd think he'd have known how to spell Earp's name. Well, he didn't. He spells it E-r-b, repeatedly . . . Some of these other Westerners did the same thing. first example is in their spelling of Tom O'Pholiard, one of Billy the Kid's boys. I've never yet seen two spellings of that name that were alike. And Dave Rudabaugh, what they didn't do to his name — "

That was as long as Eddie Slocum could hold himself.

"Goddamit, Simon!"

Lash looked up from his book. "You don't have to swear about it, Eddie. Most of these Westerners were illiterate men . . . "

"I'm not talking about that," Eddie howled. "I'm talking about you. You've quit again. Well, I quit too. I'm sick and tired of the whole goddam mess. I work like a dog. I do things that I wouldn't do for another living soul, and just about the time the going gets tough, you quit. Well, I'm through. You can take your job and — "

"Don't say it, Eddie!" Lash snapped. "Don't say it. I might get mad."

"I *am* mad!" roared Eddie Slocum. "I'm goddam good and mad. And you can go to hell. I'm through! . . . " He whirled and slammed out of the room. A moment later Lash heard the door bang downstairs.

Lash remained for a minute on the couch; then he got up, chuckling softly. "It'll do him good to let off steam." He padded out to the kitchen in his stockinged feet and began rummaging through the pantry. He looked in the refrigerator and found it empty except for a half quart of milk. On a pantry shelf, however, he found a carton of eggs and a half loaf of bread.

He fried two of the eggs and ate them with a slice of bread. He washed it down with the milk, then returned to his library. Before he could pick up his book, however, the doorbell rang. He went down the stairs and opened the door cautiously. It was a Western Union boy.

"Telegram, collect $1.95."

"Sorry," Lash said, "send it back."

He closed the door and went upstairs again; then was annoyed for the next ten minutes, wondering who the telegram was from. Probably Deacon Jones, or the Claypool Agency. If so he wasn't interested. But it might have been from someone else — perhaps from someone with an entirely new and more interesting case.

He put the Dodge City book back on a shelf and took down *The Vigilantes of Montana*, by Thomas Dimsdale. He turned the yellowed pages carefully, musing that this book would probably have to go to Eisenschiml's in the near future. It was a first edition of an extremely rare book, easily worth $200.00, which was just the amount he needed to make up Joyce Bonniwell's refund.

He scowled and was putting the book back when the telephone rang. He gave the book a last, fond caress and went to the office. He scooped up the receiver and snapped: "Hello."

"I have a long-distance call," the operator said. "From Ocelot Springs. Will you — "

"No," exclaimed Lash. "The boss isn't home. This is — the butler. Sorry." He hung up.

The phone rang again. He tried ignoring it, but it kept on ringing. He finally gave in. "Yes," he barked. "What do you want?"

"This is a station-to-station call. Here's your party . . . "

It was Sheriff Rucker, of course.

"Hello, Lash," he said. "Thought you'd be interested in developments up here."

"Well, I'm not. You're just wasting your county's money. I'm all washed up on the Bonniwell case."

"That's too bad," Sheriff Rucker replied. "I thought you'd be interested in knowing that the Barstow police dusted the entire car that they found and couldn't find a single fingerprint on it. It had been wiped clean."

"What'd you expect to find? A map?"

"As a matter of fact, they did find a map. Two of them. Road maps of Arizona and New Mexico."

"So what? Why would anyone go out to Barstow if they didn't intend going on to Arizona. It's right out in the middle

200

of the desert, isn't it?"

"Yeah, that's right; it *is* on the way to Arizona. But — would you be interested to know that Welker returned to Ocelot Springs last night and stayed at the hotel?"

"That's his tough luck."

Sheriff Rucker finally lost his patience. "You *are* in a lousy mood today, Lash. What's the matter? Mrs. Bonniwell dust you off?"

Lash gasped. "Why, you — "

"Well, she used to be your girl. I thought you were trying to take up with her again . . . "

Lash banged the receiver back on the hook, but not before he heard the desert sheriff's mocking laughter. Then he spent the next five minutes stamping about the apartment, kicking things out of his way.

He was still in his destructive mood when the doorbell rang again. Lash cried out. "What is this — the Southern Pacific Depot?"

However, he went down the stairs and opened the door. He scowled out at Oscar Loomis, who returned the scowl with a bland smile.

"Ah, Mr. Lash, may I come in a moment?"

"No, I'm busy."

"This is a business matter. It has to do with the Bonniwell thing. I have a confession . . . "

"Then go to a priest. It's his job to listen to confessions."

Loomis continued smiling, but there was a glint in his dark-brown eyes. "You're acting like a movie character, Lash," he said curtly. "Now, do you want to hear what I've got to say or don't you?"

Lash started to slam the door in the man's face, then changed his mind and pulled it wide. "Come on," he snapped and padded up the stairs to his office. Loomis followed more leisurely. When he got upstairs, Lash was already ensconced in his swivel chair, where he could look down on anyone who sat in the low-seated armchair that was obviously intended for business callers.

Loomis however, perched himself upon the arm of the chair and remained on a level with Lash.

"Well, what is it?" Lash demanded. "I told you yesterday I wasn't going to accept you as a client."

"And today I'm not interested in hiring you," Loomis retorted. "I just came to tell you that you're barking at the wrong rabbit hole. Bonniwell's death has nothing to do with — with the mink farm."

"You ought to know."

"Eh? What do you mean?"

"You said you have a confession to make. If it'll make you happier, go ahead and confess."

"All right, it's the real reason for Jim's disappearance. He came to me several days ago, told me about his jam. And it was a real jam, too. He needed the money badly and I did my damnedest to get it for him. But it was too late. In fact — I wasn't able to raise enough money, either. He needed fifty thousand, not just the twenty."

Lash sighed wearily. "So your confession amounts to this: Jim Bonniwell was swiping money from the bank and he had to put it back because the bank examiners were due? . . . "

203

Loomis looked at Lash in astonishment. "How . . . did you know?"

"A vice-president of a bank taking it on the lam — any ten-year-old kid could guess the answer. And any twelve-year-old, knowing what I know, could guess why you came here."

"Why? I told you — "

"You told me something. But not the real reason. You're a crook, Loomis. The beef is on and you're trying to get out from under, by throwing direction arrows down the side road. I know all about the mink racket, Loomis. Your part in it, too . . . "

"I don't know what — " Loomis began.

Lash cut him off short. "Shut up, Loomis. I've had San Francisco agencies covering you for days. I know that you were arrested there six months ago, that you made restitution and beat the rap. It didn't stop you from working the racket on others. And Bonniwell and Welker worked it down here. Bonniwell squeezed dollars out of the Sunset Athletic Club that hadn't seen the light of day since the Spanish-American War. The only thing I can't figure out is what the hell you crooks did with all the money. You certainly didn't waste any of it on minks."

Loomis' face had turned the color of Rocquefort cheese. "You can't prove any of that, Lash . . . "

"The hell I can't. I've already got a sucker from the club to make a deposition. Colonel Fedderson, whom Bonniwell nicked for five g's. And Plennert, the club manager, has turned stoolie. The heat's on him for shining and he wants to get out from under. You'll do ten years, Loomis."

"You're crazy, Lash!" Loomis said hoarsely. "I admit that I sold a few minks, as a personal favor to Jim, but I had nothing to do with — "

"The hell you didn't. 'Frisco has a record on you. You knew then that it was a racket and what you've done since, you did knowingly."

Loomis got up suddenly and walked to the door of the office. He stuck his neck out to see if anyone was in an adjoining room; then came back. "Look, Lash," he said in a low tone. "This is just between you and me. I've got twenty thousand dollars — "

"Which the cops'll choke out of you. And don't you try to bribe me."

"I'm not. I'm just — well, I want you to defend me. I know you're a lawyer as well as a detective — "

"I'm not," Lash cut in. "I resigned from the bar, ten years ago. I'm a detective, that's all. And I don't take swindlers as clients. Murderers, perhaps, but not cheap swindlers, or stool pigeons . . . "

Loomis ran his tongue around his dry lips. "Stool . . . "

"Stool pigeon, I said. I know why you came here. To steer me off the mink angle, on to the bank stuff and — Vincent Springer. He's skipped. Yeah, I know that. So does everyone else. He's skipped for two reasons: One, that he was in with Bonniwell on the bank shortages. Two, that he had a falling-out with Bonniwell and killed him. It's a much nicer case than a cheap swindling racket . . . and that's what you want to throw to the police.

Loomis went to the door. There he

turned and looked down at Lash. "You're a pretty crude guy, Lash. Too damn crude. That's why Joyce Bonniwell won't give you — "

Lash got up so suddenly the swivel chair went over backwards. He lunged for Loomis, but the latter was in the clear and reached the stairs in one jump. He was down them, tearing open the street door before Lash got to the stairs.

He left the door open and Lash went down to close it. He stuck out his head and saw Loomis cutting across the street to avoid Eddie Slocum, approaching the apartment.

Eddie ignored Loomis. He continued up to the door, where he said coolly, "I came to get my things. Mind?"

"Not at all, Eddie," Lash said sarcastically. "Go right up and get them."

He let Eddie crowd past him, then followed him upstairs. Eddie went to his bedroom and began throwing things around. Lash leaned against the office doorjamb.

It was five minutes before Eddie Slocum came out of the bedroom, lugging a battered suitcase. He saw Lash and said: "You can send my wages to me at the Y.M.C.A. Hotel — when you get the money."

Lash grinned and suddenly kicked at Eddie's suitcase. He had forgotten that he was in his stockinged feet and as the pain shot up into his foot, he howled and smacked Eddie Slocum in the face with his open hand.

Eddie reeled back. He dropped the suitcase and put up his hands. "All right, if you want it like this . . . "

Lash stepped forward and slapping down Eddie's hands with his left, hit the smaller man in the face with his fist. There wasn't any weight behind the blow, however. Eddie Slocum, instead of retaliating, went to pieces.

"Jeez, Chief," he cried. "This is a heluva way to break up, after all these years . . . "

"Isn't it?" Lash snarled. "Then come to your senses. There isn't a damn bit of food in the house and people are ringing the doorbell and calling me on the phone every five minutes. Get rid of them so I can have some peace."

Eddie Slocum began laughing, but his eyes were bright. Then he suddenly turned and ran into the kitchen.

Lash laughed and went to the library and put on his shoes. The telephone rang as he was lacing them and he called to Eddie Slocum.

"Eddie, answer the telephone."

Eddie trotted through the library. A moment later he came back. "It's the Price girl."

"Uh-uh," said Lash, "she called me a dirty name."

"She says it's important," Eddie hesitated. "She sounded important."

"All that I've got out of her so far, you could stick in your ear," Lash retorted. "And I spent twelve dollars on her last night — yeah, dancing in a taxi-dance joint. Tell her I can't afford to talk to her."

Eddie went off. When he returned he paused. "She was pretty sore."

"My feet are sore from dancing with her."

15

IT was noon, then. Eddie Slocum went out for food and cooked it. After lunch, Lash settled down on the couch in the library and read in Dimsdale's Vigilante book. Eddie Slocum busied himself about the apartment. Shortly after four he went out again. When he returned he was breathless.

"Chief," he cried, hoarsely. "Look at this paper. It's her! . . . ."

He thrust the open paper at Lash. There was a big headline across the paper about the European war, but Lash's eyes focused instinctively on a one-column subhead:

GIRL SLAIN IN AUTO COURT

He inhaled sharply and scanned the item below. It was evidently a rewrite of a telephoned report and told sketchily of the finding of the dead body of a red-headed girl at the auto court on

Ventura Boulevard. The girl, according to the proprietor of the court, had registered the night before, giving the name of Eva Preston.

He had heard the shot, around one o'clock while cleaning one of the cabins. He had paid no attention to it, because the court was located on the boulevard and backfiring was a continual occurrence. It was a half hour before he came to the cabin the girl occupied. Knocking and receiving no answer he had gone in . . . and found the girl dead. There was no gun in the cabin.

Lash looked up at Slocum. "Is this the address of the auto court to where you followed her?"

Slocum nodded. "And it's not a big court, either. It'd be a coincidence for two redheads to be there. And the name — look, how close it is to Evelyn Price . . . "

"All right," Lash said grimly. "Hop into the car and run down to the morgue. They'll have her there by this time. Make sure . . . "

Eddie Slocum was looking oddly at Simon Lash. A flush started at Lash's

211

throat. "I know," he said, "she wanted to tell me something on the phone. I wouldn't talk to her. I'm probably responsible for — "

"You couldn't know, Chief!" Eddie protested.

"Maybe I couldn't," Lash said. "But I fell down on the job. I won't again. I promise that, Eddie. To . . . Evelyn Price. Beat it now . . . When you come back, wait here for me. Things are going to pop."

Eddie Slocum rushed out of the apartment. Lash got his hat and coat and went into his office. He reached for the telephone and suddenly emotion gripped him so that he was compelled to rest both hands flat on the desk. He stood in that position for a long moment, staring down at the desk, his mouth slightly open. Then a shudder ran through his body and he regained control over himself.

When he picked up the telephone and spoke to the operator his voice was steady.

"I want Ocelot Springs, California. Sheriff Rucker's office."

The call was put through promptly and he heard Rucker's calm voice answering.

"This is Lash. I just want to ask one question, Rucker. Is Leon Welker at Ocelot Springs right now?"

"No, he isn't, Lash. He left here this morning. But why do you ask?"

"Just checking up. Trying to find where everyone was at one o'clock this afternoon."

"What happened?"

"A girl was killed then, a girl named Evelyn Price."

Sheriff Rucker exclaimed softly. "Why was *she* killed?"

"I don't know. But I'm going to find out. When did Welker leave Ocelot Springs?"

Rucker cleared his throat noisily. "Why, I don't know. In fact — I didn't really see him today. I told you that he'd checked in here last night. That was correct. But he wasn't in his room this morning; nor is he anywhere around town. His car's in the garage, but Welker's — disappeared."

"Then he could have been back in Hollywood at one o'clock. All right, I

213

just wanted to know."

"Does it look like his work, Lash? In that case — "

"No, I don't think it's his work. It could be, but I don't think so. My hunch is that he's gone into hiding . . . afraid the same thing'll happen to him."

"I get it!" Rucker cried. "Bonniwell . . . and everyone who was close to him. Castlemon — the girl. So, it's Springer after all."

"It looks too damn much like Springer!" Lash snapped. "There's still Loomis, remember, and — "

"And who . . . Lord, it couldn't be a woman!"

"Why not? A woman could fire a gun as well as a man."

"But it doesn't make sense, Lash. Admit she was sore at the redhead and killed Castlemon because he knew what was what, why would she kill Bonniwell — before he got the money from Loomis? . . . "

The sheriff was referring to Drusilla Denham. Lash had been thinking of another woman, Joyce Bonniwell. Joyce Bonniwell, whose husband had been unfaithful, who had left her without any money . . . and was worth a hundred thousand dollars, dead.

Could Joyce Bonniwell kill two men and a woman? Simon Lash asked himself the question and dared not answer it. He had known Joyce Bonniwell when she had been Joyce Prentice, ten years younger. He had known her well . . . and then she had married Jim Bonniwell.

Well, perhaps she had loved Jim Bonniwell, who even then was cashier of the Sheridan National Bank and was worth, privately, well over a hundred thousand dollars. It is just as easy to love a wealthy man as a poor one. And it is a lot easier to marry him.

Lash paced the floor of the apartment, from the library to the office and the front windows overlooking the street. A scowl outside and then back again. After ten minutes he could stand it no longer. He got his hat and coat and left the apartment.

Once on the street he almost ran to Sunset Boulevard to catch a cab. He sent it dashing through the Sunset strip, lined with shops and offices of motion-picture

215

agents, into Beverly Hills.

The maid with the face that scared children let him into Joyce Bonniwell's house and Joyce came in from the yard.

"Simon!" she exclaimed when she saw his grim face. "What's happened?"

He said: "You've heard about Ben Castlemon?"

"Yes. I read about it in the papers. It's horrible. I can't understand for the life of me — "

"Neither can I. But that isn't all. That little redheaded girl who had the apartment on Wilshire with — "

She winced. "Must you, Simon?"

"I must. That girl — her name was Evelyn Price, and she was a very real girl regardless of what you think that girl was murdered, just a little while ago."

"Oh!" Joyce cried, inhaling sharply. "That's — "

"Horrible, you said before."

She stared at him, her blue eyes wide. "Simon," she said in a tone of awe, "what are you driving at? Your attitude . . . I don't like it."

"I don't like yours, Joyce," he told her evenly. "I haven't liked it from the start.

You hired me to hound that girl. Because of me, she is dead right now. She never had a chance. I saw her last night. She knew all about Bonniwell, that he was no good, that he would throw her over when he got tired of her. She didn't care. Well, she *did* care. But she wasn't complaining. She wasn't asking much . . . of life. And she got . . . death!"

"But why blame me, Simon?" Joyce cried. "I said I was sorry. I didn't wish her any harm. You ought to know that — "

"I don't know it, Joyce!" Lash cut in curtly. "I don't know it at all. I only know that right from the start, when I got on that girl's trail, her troubles began. Already — " He stopped and a glint came into his eyes. "Already the girl was being shadowed from another angle. Say . . . if I thought that you and — "

"What are you talking about, Simon?" Joyce screamed hysterically. "Me and who? . . . "

"And Vincent Springer. He'd hired the Otis Agency to shadow that girl. There are twenty detective agencies in the city. How'd he happen to pick the

217

same outfit you'd used — and the very same operator, Burkhart?"

The malignancy of Lash's tone shocked Joyce out of her hysteria. "Are you mad, Simon? It was Vincent who suggested the Otis Agency to me. I asked him about Jim — what to do. He advised employing a detective agency and recommended the Otis Agency, who he said had done some work for the bank . . . "

Lash's suspicion did not subside. "I can't check that, because Springer's gone. But I don't like the pattern. I don't like it at all."

"Do you think I like anything about it?" Joyce cried. "I've lost everything I ever had, everything that — "

"And you're gaining a hundred thousand dollars!" Lash said harshly.

She flinched as if he had struck her in the face and then he whirled and left her house.

Outside, he strode to Sunset Boulevard and turned east. He walked to the line dividing Beverly Hills and West Hollywood before he had calmed sufficiently to step into a taxi.

Eddie Slocum had returned to the

apartment when Lash reached it. He nodded soberly.

"It was her, all right."

Although he had been certain for two hours, Lash was suddenly assailed by an overwhelming sense of depression. He started for the library, but Eddie called to him:'

"Wait, Chief! Here are a couple of things . . . " He thrust a folded newspaper at Lash.

The latter took it and glanced at the headline:

MURDER SUSPECT ELUDES POLICE

Below was a melodramatic account of the hunt for Drusilla Denham. According to the police statement, just issued, a dragnet had been spread for the platinum blonde, after the discovery of Bonniwell's deserted car in Barstow.

A Los Angeles-bound bus driver, reaching the end of his run and learning of the search, reported that a girl answering Drusilla's description, had traveled in his bus from Barstow to Pasadena. The police, three hours behind the girl, descended upon Pasadena and learned that a platinum blonde had just purchased a brand new, yellow Packard coupé. She had given the name of Ella Mason, and the license had been obtained for her in that name by the local automobile dealer.

The girl had driven the car out of the dealer's place — and that was the last that was seen of either the girl or the car. The police admitted their failure, but maintained stoutly that the girl would be apprehended within 'a few hours.' They pointed out that they had the license number of the girl's car. She could not drive very long on any highway without a state trooper or filling station operator seeing it. The license number was given in the paper — 9 V 44-36.

Eddie Slocum said, "I got to thinking how the killer located the girl at the auto court. He must have followed her — and me — from here."

Lash said, "Of course! I knew that."

"Uh-huh, but there wasn't anyone around outside when we left here. I looked."

Lash looked sharply at his assistant.

"What're you getting at, Eddie?"

"Just this. How'd the fella know the other night that only you were home when he took a shot at you?"

"Spare me the deductions, Eddie," Lash said harshly. "If you've got something, spill it."

"It's the rooming house across the street. You want to take a look at it?"

Lash started for the stairs. "Come on!"

They crossed the street to the yellow-stuccoed two-story house, that had a sign beside the front door: "Rooms." Lash pressed the doorbell impatiently and a blowsy-looking woman answered his ring.

"My name's Lash. I live across the street."

"Oh, the detective man. What can? — "

"Someone's been spying on me," Lash said curtly. "I think he lives over here."

"Here, Mr. Lash? Oh, that couldn't be. All my roomers are such nice men."

"How many have you got?"

"Only five right now. There's Mr. Tilman, the insurance man, Mr. Schnabel, who works at the A & P Grocery, and — "

221

"Which ones have front rooms?"

"Why, only Mr. Tilman now. Of course there's that nice Mr. Vedder, but he was here only such a little while — "

"When did he move in?" Lash demanded harshly. "And when did he leave?"

"Why, he only stayed two days. He left this morning. Or . . . it might have been last night."

"You don't know when?"

"Well, not exactly. You see, he paid a week's rent in advance and this morning when I went to clean up his room — he was gone. Took all his luggage."

"Let me see his room."

The landlady took them to a front bedroom, on the second floor, a rather large room. Lash went immediately to the front windows and muttered under his breath.

"He didn't even need a spyglass. Look, Eddie. You can see the fountain pen on my desk." He whirled upon the rooming-house keeper.

"This man who called himself Vedder, what did he look like?"

"Why, he was a very nice gentleman.

Distinguished-looking."

"About forty-five years old?"

"Perhaps he was, although he looked a little younger. He was a very good dresser."

Lash said to Slocum: "If there's anything I hate, it's calling on the police for help. But dusting an entire room for prints is too much for us. Mrs . . . uh, Madam, may I use your telephone?"

"Of course, Mr. Lash, but — I don't understand about the police. There wasn't anything — wrong about Mr. Vedder, was there?"

"Nothing," said Lash, "nothing except that he's murdered three people in the last three days."

The woman said "*Eeek!*" and started to keel over. Eddie Slocum caught her.

"She's fainted!" he cried.

"Put her on the bed. She'll come round. I've got to telephone the cops."

Lash strode out of the bedroom. On the lower floor he found a hall telephone. "I want the Fairfax Police Station," he said crisply, after dialing the operator.

When he got the station, he asked for

223

Lieutenant Hayden and got him after a moment. "Lash talking," he said then. "Simon Lash. I've got something that'll interest you. Bring a fingerprint man along with you. With all his gadgets."

He hung up and went across the street to his own apartment. The police car came within five minutes, siren screaming. Lash cursed as people began popping out of buildings up and down Harper Avenue. The car drew up to the curb and two men piled out.

Lash met them at his door. "Where's the body?" the detective lieutenant cried.

"There isn't any," Lash scowled, "but there's a room across the street I'd like you to dust for fingerprints."

"What the hell!" the lieutenant protested. "Since when d'you think we work for private dicks?"

"You'll be interested in these fingerprints."

"Why?"

"Because the man who made them killed a girl today — the girl who was murdered at the auto court out on Ventura."

The lieutenant exclaimed. "What do you know about that?"

"More than you do — so far. That girl is the redhead who was up here the other night. She was followed when she left here. Identify those prints across the street and you've got a murderer — a triple murderer!"

The lieutenant looked steadily at Lash for a moment, then turned and ran across the street. His fingerprint man followed him at a more sedate pace.

16

LASH went up to his office and stood at the window looking across the street until Eddie Slocum came out of the rooming house. When he came into the apartment he shook his head. "The old girl came to and is hollering bloody murder. Says you're a menace to the neighborhood."

"I didn't house a murderer for three days," Lash retorted. He stared morosely out of the window. "This may break the case. They oughtn't to have any trouble getting prints of Springer, Loomis and Welker, and the ones over there ought to match one of them."

"And we haven't got a client," Eddie Slocum said softly. "What books are going next?"

"Maybe I'll have to sell the whole damn bunch and get into some other racket." Lash swore. "Damn, I might even have to go back into law and I can't think of anything I'd rather not do than that."

"Mm," said Eddie. "You'll need a process server and — " he grinned — "a good ambulance chaser. I think I'll stick around."

"Hollywood Park'll be looking for you, Eddie . . . Here comes the lieutenant. He looks sore about something."

The detective pounded heavily up the steps. When he came into the office he was glowering. "Are you kidding someone, Lash? That room's been gone over with a wet rag."

Lash inhaled softly. "Everything?"

"I dunno yet. Julius isn't finished. But there certainly aren't any prints on the furniture. Julius is trying the closet doorknobs and the out-of-the-way spots. But I'm not holding out any hopes."

Lash shook his head. "It's been that way all along. Tell me, what progress are the police making in their search for Drusilla Denham?"

"None. It begins to look like she dug a hole in the Mojave Desert and drove herself and the car into the hole. They're working on Springer now . . . Umm, is it your idea that the man across the street was Springer?"

"He answers the description. But Welker and Loomis are close enough too. Why don't you get pictures of all of them and show them to the landlady across the street?"

"Can't. Welker's disappeared. That desert sheriff sent a teletype message to headquarters to look out for him. For that matter, this Loomis lad has checked out of the Hollywood-Wilson without leaving a forwarding address."

"Looks like they've all run into their holes," Lash observed.

The detective looked suspiciously at Lash. "I've got me an itching hunch that you know a heluva lot more about this business than you've let on so far. Come on, spill it. I can make you talk, you know."

"You tried that the other night."

"Things was different then. We were merely doing a favor for an outside sheriff. But this girl's killing was here in our territory . . ."

"I identified her for you, didn't I? That's something."

The lieutenant grunted. "I'm suspicious of that, too."

"Identify her yourself, then. You saw the girl here the other night. Go down to the morgue — "

"I wasn't suspicious of that part. It's your reason for tipping me off. Just like the fingerprints across the street. You were pretty damn sure we wouldn't find any."

"On the contrary, I'm greatly disappointed. Finding those prints would have washed up this case."

"Except for catching Vincent Springer. And Drusilla Denham."

"Those are minor details."

"Oh yeah? I suppose you could do it?"

"If I had the incentive. And the facilities of the police department. You've got motorcycle policemen patrolling all the highways, haven't you?"

The doorbell rang and the fingerprint man came up the stairs. He shook his head. "I dusted everything, Lieutenant. Not a single print."

The detective-lieutenant swore without enthusiasm. "That's the breaks for you. If you'd found only one print, Julius, I coulda got my picture in the paper."

229

"Endorse Honeybunch Soap and you can get on the radio," Lash said sarcastically.

The detective said some words that made Lash wince and took his departure. The fingerprint man trotted after his superior.

When they had gone Lash took a quick turn about the office, then plopped himself down in the swivel chair. "That was cutting it pretty fine, Eddie. How'd he know we wouldn't see *him*?"

"If you ask me," said Eddie Slocum. "It isn't Springer at all. It's Loomis or Welker. They were in and out of here and whichever one it was just figured he'd bluff that he was coming here if one of us should have run into him."

"I can't figure out a motive for Welker or Loomis," said Lash. "At least not a strong enough one. That mink business was pretty well shot. The heat was on at the Sunset Club and it was just a matter of days before the thing exploded. Would either Loomis or Welker murder, just to dodge a five-year rap? For that matter, there wasn't anything holding them around. Loomis has no strings tying him down. Welker probably has a wife in every city. Do you know, so far, we haven't learned a single important fact about Welker? Where he makes his headquarters, what he did before he popped into the mink racket?"

"A mystery man, eh?"

"Not necessarily. He's just an ordinary bird of passage. Gold bricks in Iowa, mining stocks in Colorado, mink in California. A sharpshooter who skims off a little cream here and digests it there. Loomis is more substantial."

"I see what you mean, Chief. He couldn't run out as easy as Welker. That goes for Springer, too. Only twice as much. He's a big shot. Been around here a long time."

"That's why I don't believe he had anything to do with the mink racket. Unless his friendship for Jim Bonniwell dragged him into it. I tell you what I'd like you to do, Eddie. Run over and talk to this bank-teller friend of yours. See if you can't get an advance tip on how the books are stacking up."

"Huh? You think they're going over them?"

"That's a cinch. The minute Springer's name was mentioned in the same breath with murder, the bank examiners went hopping over to the Sheridan National. They may not be talking yet, but the teller ought to be able to make a guess, from their actions around the bank."

"I think you've got something there. I'll see what I can smell out."

"Fine, but don't stay too long. I've got a funny feeling that something's going to break and I wouldn't be a bit surprised if we're in the middle of it."

Slocum was startled. "Say, you don't think . . . " He went to a closet and rummaged about in it for a moment. Finally he produced a nickel-plated .38 caliber revolver. "Maybe you better keep this handy. He might come back and make another try . . . "

Lash grimaced. "Put that thing away, Eddie. You know I don't like guns."

Slocum spun the cylinder. "Well, you know where it is, in case . . . " He returned the gun back into the closet and went out of the apartment.

When Eddie had gone, Lash leaned back in the chair and clasped his hands behind the back of his head. He sighed wearily and closed his eyes. He hadn't slept well the last couple of nights.

The events of the last three days churned in his mind. And suddenly something exploded in his brain; his eyes popped wide open.

Reaching across the desk he pulled forward a pad of paper. He picked up a pencil and began writing names on the paper, the names of the various actors in the drama, listing them in the sequence in which each had made entry.

He wrote:

Joyce Bonniwell
Jim Bonniwell
Vincent Springer
Evelyn Price
Ben Castlemon
Leon Welker
Oscar Loomis
Drusilla Denham

He stared at the list a moment, then struck out the names of Jim Bonniwell, Ben Castlemon and Evelyn Price.

He drew an arrow in front of the name

Vincent Springer, then added a curved tail and brought it down to the name of Drusilla Denham. He studied the two names for a moment; then made a new list of three names:

Jim Bonniwell
Ben Castlemon
Evelyn Price

Suddenly he caught his breath and lunged for the telephone. Dialing the operator, he snapped: "I want long distance . . . San Francisco. The Deacon Jones Detective Agency. Wait a minute — the name isn't Deacon. It's Amos Jones . . . All right, I'll hang on."

Less than two minutes later, the smooth voice of Deacon Jones purred: "That you, Simon Lash, I was just about to send you a telegram. You haven't sent me that additional fifty I asked for."

"Damn you, Deacon!" Lash snapped. "You haven't given me ten dollars' worth of information. You didn't tell me one thing that I didn't already know about Oscar Loomis."

Deacon Jones began whining. "Oh, come now, Lash. I worked like a dog getting that information. That stuff about him having worked a con game six months ago wasn't even on the police blotter . . ."

"*I* knew it," Lash retorted, "and I haven't been in 'Frisco in six years. What I really wanted to know about Loomis, you didn't tell me. I wanted a character sketch of him. Is he a gay dog? Does he like his women and liquor?"

"I don't know what he does when he's away from home," complained the Deacon. "Naturally he behaves himself pretty well around here. His wife keeps him in line — "

"His wife!" cried Lash. "You mean — he's married?"

"Of course, didn't I tell you? He married his boss' daughter, eight years ago. They've got three children."

"Why, you blithering, blundering, stupid oaf!" Lash howled. "That's the most important thing in the whole goddam case and you neglected to tell me. Why, you . . . "

He started off again, but Deacon Jones

235

screamed into the phone: "Why didn't you tell me what you wanted? I thought you were working on the Bonniwell case. What has Loomis' domestic status got to do with the Bonniwell case? . . . "

"Oh!" groaned Lash. He slammed the receiver on the hook and pushed back his chair. Springing to his feet, he ran around his desk and snatched his hat from the hat tree just inside the door.

He was at the head of the stairs, when he changed his mind and ran back into the office. He lost thirty-two minutes then hunting the telephone directory. He finally found it and dialed a number. After a moment a woman's voice answered, "Villa Del Mar."

"Hello," Lash said, "this is the police department — "

"The police department?" shrieked the woman's voice. "What . . . what do you want?"

"We are making a routine checkup on a former tenant of yours, Mrs. Oscar Loomis . . . "

"Oh!" There was sudden relief in the woman's voice. "Why, she's not living here any more. There was an officer here the day before yesterday. I told him all about it . . . "

"I know, I know," Lash said patiently. "It isn't that — it's — well, did you see the picture in the newspapers? The picture of James Bonniwell, who . . . "

"Yes, I saw it, but they made a mistake. They said the Mr. Loomis who lived at my place was really named Bonniwell. But that wasn't Mr. Loomis' picture at all. Of course I only saw Mr. Loomis two or three times and never talked much with him, but I'm pretty sure the picture they printed of Mr. Bonniwell wasn't Mr. Loomis. I mean, Mr. Loomis wasn't Mr. Bonniwell . . . Oh! Now I'm confused . . . "

"It wasn't the picture of the man you knew as Loomis? Is that it?" Lash asked sharply.

"That's right. I understand, of course, that Mr. Loomis, I mean Mr. Bonniwell, was using a different name, but still that picture — well, the man *I* knew as Mr. Loomis was thinner in the face . . . "

"Thanks," said Lash. "That's exactly what I wanted to know."

He hung up just as the doorbell rang.

He went down and opened the door. Joyce Bonniwell came in.

"I was just going to call you," Lash exclaimed. "I think I've got a break on the case."

She said dully. "A break? I've just had one myself. A bad one."

He led the way into the office. When he faced her he saw that her face was sagging. He moistened his lips and his eyes narrowed.

"I'll hear yours first," he said.

Her red lips twisted. They were over-rouged, in vivid contrast to her over-powdered face. "I told you the other day that I'd made a claim for Jim's insurance . . ."

"Yes," he said, "a hundred thousand dollars' worth. What's the matter; didn't he have that much?"

"He *had* it," she replied. "Only he borrowed on it — up to the last dollar they would allow him. So . . ." She laughed harshly. "So he beat me, even in the end!"

He stared at her for a moment; then his lip curled contemptuously. "They're not going to pay you . . . anything?"

"Practically nothing. Around fifteen hundred dollars. How long do you think that will last me?"

"About a month," he said. "But your nice mink coat will bring a couple of thousand. And your jewelry — "

"Most of it's gone," she said. "The house is mortgaged to the limit. So is the furniture. Jim got everything. If I'd known . . . "

"You'd have given him hell, eh?"

"You know, Simon," she said wearily. "Even your sarcasm doesn't affect me, now."

"Then, why'd you come here?"

She shrugged her shapely shoulders.

"I guess I had to tell someone. Besides, I thought — "

"What?"

"You mentioned something about returning that money. The five hundred . . . I guess I'll be able to use it, now."

Lash laughed humorlessly. "I've spent most of it. But don't worry, you'll get it back. I'll sell some of my books."

She regarded him curiously. "You mean? . . . Why, I was under the impression that you were — "

239

"Well-heeled? Your informant was in error. I don't handle a dozen cases in a year. Besides, my books — "

She laughed. "That's really funny. Why, you're poorer than I am."

"No," he said. "I'm rich compared to you. You see, money doesn't mean a damn to me. It does to you."

She thought about that a moment. "I guess it does, Simon. I've had it too long. Well, I won't bother you again with my troubles." She started for the door.

"Wait a minute. I haven't given you my news. It may make you feel a little better about Bonniwell. I was wrong about him and the Price girl. It wasn't Bonniwell who had the apartment with her."

"What?"

"It was Oscar Loomis."

She stared at him. "But Oscar's married! . . . "

"So was Bonniwell. Of course, he didn't have the three children that Loomis has, but — "

He stopped. Color was flooding her face. Her lips moved silently for an instant; then she shook her head and walked out of the office.

Lash listened until he heard the door close downstairs. Then he laughed. It was a bitter laugh, but there was a note of relief in it. And just the trace of a sob.

★ ★ ★

When Eddie Slocum returned to the apartment a half hour later he found Lash with his hat and coat on and a valise standing at the head of the stairs.

"Going on a trip, Chief?" he asked in surprise.

Lash made an impatient gesture. "Maybe. What'd you find out?

Eddie nodded. "They're not finished checking up yet, but there's plenty missing. It might run into the hundreds of thousands . . . "

"I thought so," Lash snarled. "That mink business was chicken feed. All right, I'm going to finish it up. Is the car gassed?"

"It's got almost a full tank. Uh . . . how long you going to be gone?"

"Maybe two or three days. I'm going to find Vincent Springer."

Eddie inhaled softly. "You know where he is?"

"No. But I figure Drusilla Denham does . . ."

"But you don't know where *she* is?" cried Eddie Slocum.

"I think I can find her." Lash picked up the valise and carried it out to the car. He stowed it away in the luggage compartment; when he came around to climb into the car Eddie was putting the revolver in the glove compartment.

A year ago Lash had pursued, on behalf of a client, a man equipped with an expensive automobile. He had been ignominiously left behind and, smarting because of it, had used a part of his next fee in having certain things done to his modest little car.

It was a light coupé and looked pretty much the worse for wear. A close observer would have noticed, however, that the car had excellent rubber all around and that in traffic, it usually got first across the intersection.

What it did on a straightaway road, unencumbered with highway police, only Lash and Eddie Slocum knew. Rather, they only suspected, for as yet neither had had occasion to let the car out to its limit.

He said: "You can't tell . . . Wish I could go along, to try out the car. Those desert roads are the flattest and straightest in the country."

"You're needed here, Eddie. There are loose ends that have to be tied up . . . and I may be guessing wrong. I want you to see what Joyce Bonniwell does. If you can't handle it yourself, get Otis to stake out a man. Mm . . . Better get Otis; you stick by the telephone."

Eddie nodded. "Okay, Simon." He watched Lash drive off.

Lash drove circumspectly enough; down Sunset to Los Feliz, then out to Colorado, which took him through Glendale and Pasadena.

17

LEAVING Pasadena, Lash kept the coupé rolling at steady forty miles per hour through the orange-growing centers of Monrovia, Azusa and Fontana. The highway was patrolled and while he could have hit it up in stretches, the risk involved, with its resultant delay, was not worth while. Once through San Bernardino, however, he let his foot rest heavier on the gas pedal and the little coupé took the long grade up Cajon Pass with a vigor that was satisfying to Lash.

Falling down into the desert the coupé went down so swiftly that Lash almost missed a couple of the turns and was compelled to brake.

Heat waves shimmered on the desert road and within ten minutes of leaving the mountains Lash had to stop the car, remove his coat and loosen his shirt collar. By the time he drove into the town of Victorville he was gasping.

And now it was time for him to start work. This was a hundred miles from Los Angeles. The next town of any consequence was Barstow, fifty miles away. Before venturing on such a long jump through desert, a driver looks at his gasoline . . . and water.

Lash's gas tank was half empty. He got it filled at the first filling station and while the man was putting it in he got out of the car and said casually:

"This is one heluva day to drive through the desert. How was it yesterday?"

"Hotter," replied the attendant shortly.

"You don't say!" Lash exclaimed. "Wonder how my sister stood it? She drove through — on her way to Las Vegas."

The man finished with the gasoline. "I better check the oil and water."

Lash followed him around. "Maybe you saw my sister, yesterday. A swell-looking blond — a platinum blonde, driving a brand-new car."

The attendant pulled out the oil stick and shoved it back again. "Oil's okay . . . And so's the water."

"You'd have noticed my sister if she'd

stopped here," Lash persisted, as he fumbled for money.

The attendant sighed. "Look, Mister, we have newspapers even out here. The dame you're talking about is Drusilla Denham . . . and you're a dick, eh?"

"That's right," Lash replied, taken aback.

"Fine, then you stop up the street at the Excello station. She got gas there. And it wasn't yesterday. It was only an hour ago. Although, if you ask me, Nick Costello's a liar."

Lash went to the Excello Station. Nick Costello beamed when Lash told him the purpose of his inquiry. "Yes, sir, I saw her. She was a pippin. I thought she was some movie actress at first. Then I remembered reading about her in the paper . . . "

"What time was it when she stopped here?"

"Right around five o'clock. Maybe a few minutes after. The troopers came around five thirty. They lit right out after her. I ain't heard that they caught her, though."

"They went down 66, toward Barstow?"

"It's the only way they *can* go."

"Why? There are other roads."

"Not across the desert, there ain't."

"What makes you think she was going to cross the desert?"

"Why, uh, she asked. I mean, how was the weather at night? Was there much traffic and etcetry."

Lash nodded. It was apparent that Drusilla Denham had deliberately planted the idea of desert travel in the filling station man's mind. That meant she wasn't going across the desert.

Or did it?

The way Nick, the gas station attendant, put it, it sounded like she had questioned him directly. Yet, it might not have been that way at all. She might have been more subtle . . . and she might not have asked about road conditions at all. The questions might have been put into Nick's mouth, by the state police . . . Or his own imagination. That the man was enjoying his sudden importance was apparent.

Lash started out on the Barstow road, but went only a few miles before stopping his car to study his road map.

Yes, the roads were plainly marked. Highway 66 went to Barstow. It was the only road leading in that direction. But at Barstow Highway 66 turned south and east to Needles and Arizona. Also at Barstow, Highway 91 began its northeasterward fork across the desert, to Las Vegas, Nevada, where it met Highway 93, which in turn went south, through Boulder City, Boulder Dam and into Arizona, joining Highway 66 at Kingman. Those were the main roads, but here and there in the desert, roads that were no more than trails cut across the highways. They could be traveled by a desperate driver. Drusilla Denham was desperate.

Highway 66, through Needles, was the direct route to Arizona. A fugitive, not knowing the country, would take that road. An experienced traveler would choose Highway 91, at Barstow, knowing that although twenty-five miles longer, it was actually the quicker road. The mountain grades on it were easier.

The desperate fugitive would use neither Highways 91 nor 66.

Lash debated the matter with himself

for several minutes, then decided to risk everything on a gamble. He turned back to Victorville, picked up State Highway Number 18 and drove twenty miles to Lucerne Valley. Highway 18 still continued southward here, but slanting away from it, eastward, was a desert road, leading into the bleak wastes of the Mojave. There were names on the map, Old Woman Springs, Rock Corral, Warren's Well.

Lash had traveled on the desert before. He was not fooled by those names. They were not towns, or even hamlets. Lucky for him, if there was a gasoline pump or even a store at those places. They were specks on the desert; not even to be called oases, for the American desert dweller does not require an oasis. A Joshua palm is enough for him.

Lash sent the car hurtling through the darkness. As yet, there was no moon and his powerful headlights lit up the entire countryside ahead. As it was, he missed the first of the desert oases. The second, Rock Corral, showed up as a few dark shadows on either side of the road and he didn't even bother to slacken his speed for them. He continued on to Warren's Well, which was on the paved road to Twenty-nine Palms, a resort. He drove the twenty-three miles of paved road in eighteen minutes flat, then at the first light of a filling station stopped the car, to let the overheated motor rest a moment.

He had more gasoline put into the tank, and while the man was doing the job, questioned him closely. Yes, a lot of cars drove by at night. Not one in a hundred stopped. No, he paid no attention to the passing cars.

No yellow Packard had stopped; he had seen none pass. Disappointed, Lash got into the car and heading east started on a long stretch of fifty miles, which did not even show a 'well' on the map. He saw not a single, solitary light on that trip.

The road was terrible. Even with his light, high-powered car and reckless driving it took him an hour and a half to drive the fifty miles. When he finally reached the little town of Amboy, he was again on Highway 66. If he was guessing right, the fugitive would drive twelve miles on the pavement, to Cadiz, then cut off again down a forty-nine-mile stretch of desert road to the Colorado River Aqueduct.

The road was a little better than the previous one and Lash made fairly good time. Landing on the pavement he did not stop, but drove east toward the Colorado River, fifty miles away. He made the trip in forty minutes, reaching the little town of Earp — named after the famous frontier marshal, Wyatt Earp — shortly before eleven.

A gasoline station was open. Lash got more gas and questioned the operator and at last got a glimmer of hope. The man didn't remember any new Packard coupé — and felt sure he would have if one had stopped — but he did recall selling gasoline to an uncommonly beautiful young woman. Unfortunately it had been dark and he hadn't been able to distinguish the color of her hair, but he thought it light.

That had been at ten o'clock. If it was Drusilla Denham, Lash was but an hour and a half behind her.

He studied his road map. Across the

Colorado River was Arizona. Highway 72, paved part way, led to U.S. Highway 60, forty miles away. Highway 60 was the through route, leading to Phoenix, Tucson and the most populous sections of Arizona.

Highway 60, however, also joined with Highway 89, which ran north to Prescott and Highway 66, the main transcontinental highway. A normal traveler, planning a coast-to-coast trip, would invariably travel on Highway 66. So would a fugitive — after pursuit was no longer feared, for 66 was the best road, as well as the shortest to eastern points.

If Lash were a fugitive he would now cut up to Highway 66, reaching it somewhere in the center of the State, either at Williams or Flagstaff. Or to be absolutely safe, at Winslow.

With a full tank of gasoline he started up the motor, took a deep breath and headed into Arizona. Once the little town of Parker was left behind, he drove as he had never driven before, sending the car hurtling up mountain grades, screaming around hairpin turns and finally dropping down into the flat stretches, in excess of eighty miles an hour. He cut down to seventy on the gravel stretches, but reaching Highway 60 he really let the car out. It swished over the desert road at better than ninety miles an hour. He reached Wickenburg at ten minutes to one, Prescott at twenty to two and Williams at three o'clock sharp.

He was groggy-eyed then, and his muscles quivered from the strain. He went into an all-night restaurant, had two cups of coffee in quick succession, then got a handful of dimes and played one of the slot machines near the door. He lost two dollars and engaged the waiter in conversation. No, the man hadn't heard of Drusilla Denham. Women stopped here at night sometimes, but they were usually tourists. You could always tell a tourist. They wore pants, a lot of them did. And they were either timid little ladies, or hard-boiled, fat dames, or horse-faced schoolma'ams, going to see Hollywood.

The waiter gave them their coffee, sometimes a sandwich and that was that.

"S'funny," remarked the highway sage,

"a dame'll pay for her gas but try to work the come-on stuff with a ginzo in a restaurant for her grub. Why do you suppose that is? . . . "

Lash didn't answer. The door of the restaurant opened and a girl came in. She wore blue slacks, a tan shirt and had a wind scarf twisted about her head, entirely concealing her hair. She walked to the counter and straddled a stool.

"Cup of coffee, please," she said.

18

LASH nodded to the waiter and went out. He had parked his car a few feet up the street. Walking to it, he passed a coupé of considerable vintage. Due to the contraction of hot metal, it was groaning and wheezing. In the dim light shed by the restaurant window he saw that the car had California plates.

He stuck his head into the car, by the wheel. The dashboard lights were out, but striking a match he saw that the water registered well over 200, indicating that the old car had been crowded hard.

Lash was tempted to search the car, but knew that he didn't have the time. He went to his own car, started up the motor and backed the car across the pavement into the lee of a darkened filling station.

With the lights out, then, and the motor quiet, he waited.

It was only a minute or two. The girl

came out of the restaurant, stood in front of it for an instant, then hurried to her car. She got in, switched on the lights and started the motor. Then she backed a few feet and swung out forward upon the road.

The speed with which the car went shooting out of Williams surprised Lash, but he waited until the single taillight had made a turn in the road, before he sent his own car in pursuit. He ran through the town without putting on his lights, then making the turn the other car had made, switched on his lights.

He picked up the car ahead, almost a half mile away. He smiled grimly. If the girl was just a casual tourist she was in for the scare of her life. He stepped hard on the gas pedal and was slammed back against the seat cushions.

He held the speedometer at seventy, saw that he was making no gain, on an uphill drive, and knew that the girl was giving her old car all that it had. She didn't want anyone to come up behind her, not on one of the lonesomest stretches of road in the world, at three o'clock in the morning.

The taillight disappeared to the right and Lash pressed heavier on the accelerator. His stepped-up motor began to purr deeply.

Another straightaway and he looked at the speedometer; seventy-eight and he had gained considerably. The grade ahead was steep and Lash knew that the girl's car had reached its limit. The girl must have known that she could not outrun Lash's car, for suddenly she slackened speed. Lash eased off his own, until he was going no more than thirty-five.

He remained a quarter of a mile behind the other car. They kept those positions for almost a mile, when the girl, reaching a level stretch, let her car out again. Lash, chuckling wickedly, decided to give her a real thrill.

He increased his speed until he was hurtling along at better than eighty. He closed up the distance between himself and the girl's car to less than two hundred feet, eased off and held it there.

They were doing between seventy-five and eighty on a rather rough road, which was fast traveling, and undoubtedly the straightaway limit of the other car.

The girl must have been pretty desperate by now. She scarcely slowed for the turns, crowded her ancient car on the grades and on the straight stretches let it out for everything it had. Lash hugged her taillight.

They kept that up until they reached Flagstaff, almost seven thousand feet above sea level, some thirty miles from Williams. Flagstaff was a fair-sized town and it was the place for the girl to make her stand. There were police here; restaurants and tourist homes had lights.

The girl did stop, parallel to the curb in front of the Santa Fé Depot. Lash parked his car a hundred feet behind, switched off his lights. He waited for the girl to climb out of her car.

She didn't, however. She remained in the car for five minutes; then started off. She rolled easily through Flagstaff at a modest thirty miles, made the wide turn that brought San Francisco Peak to her left, and then — then she pulled to the shoulder of the road and stopped.

Lash's first reaction was to slam on

the brakes, but then he stepped on the gas and swung past the other car. He slackened speed instantly, looking in the rear-vision mirror. The girl was making a quick U turn.

Lash swore, slammed on the brakes and also made the turn. If she wanted a showdown, very well.

But the girl didn't go back to Flagstaff. Instead of continuing on the pavement she suddenly swung to the left on a graveled road that Lash had not noticed before.

He stopped his car, flashed on his lights to bright and then switched them off altogether. In the moment of brightness he saw that the graveled road ran straight for a long stretch.

Quickly he unfolded his map. Yes, it showed a graveled road here. It ran down alongside of Mormon Lake, where it met another graveled road, then led back on another side of a triangle to Highway 66. Each side of the triangle measured about thirty miles, a total of sixty. The same distance on Highway 66 was no more than thirty miles.

The girl seemed to prefer the lonely,

less-traveled road.

Lash bit his lip. Ahead, the taillight of the girl's car was almost out of sight. He shifted into second, sent the car leaping forward. In high, he switched on his lights. She had about a mile start on him. Inside of two minutes he had cut the distance in half, then halved it again.

When he got up to within a hundred yards of her, he eased off. He would play the game a little while longer, put the fear of the devil into her heart. She knew that he was pursuing her now. She had herself selected the scene for the showdown.

She called for it sooner than he expected. It came without warning. Driving at better than sixty miles an hour she began braking. The operation raised a tremendous cloud of dust. Lash had to swing wide to make sure he would not bump her from the rear.

He brought his car to a stop only a few feet ahead of hers, jerked on the emergency brake and started opening the door at his side, to climb out.

He heard shoes scrape on gravel and then — a sharp explosion, followed instantly by another. Lash ducked involuntarily, expecting glass to shatter over him.

None did, but after a moment he heard a loud hissing sound. A tire!

He lunged for the glove compartment of his car, got it open and groped for the revolver Eddie Slocum had stowed away for him. It was a moment before he found it and then when he was swinging it through the window at his side, the girl's car was shooting past him. He had a fleeting glimpse of her scarf-swathed face and could have shot her, then.

But he didn't. And then she was gone. He climbed out of his car, and standing in the middle of the road, fired two shots after her. He held the gun down to the road, however, in a rather vain attempt to hit one of her tires. He missed, of course.

And then it was no use firing at all. The girl's car was out of range.

He walked around to the rear of his car and cursed luridly. She had not fired two shots at one tire, no, indeed. One bullet, one tire. Both rear tires were flat . . . and Lash had but one spare!

He walked back to the wheel and looked at his speedometer. Was he just a mile or two out of Flagstaff, or was it five miles? He'd forgotten to look at the mileage indicator.

Well, there was no use standing there. She was gone. Lash climbed back into his car and made an awkward U turn on two flat tires. He would cut them to ribbons, of course, might even injure the rims, but it was a cinch that if he walked back to Flagstaff, returned with a mechanic and tires, he was simply out of it.

His only chance was to keep the wasted time down to the minimum. So he drove back on the rims. It was six miles to Flagstaff and it took him twenty-five minutes to cover the distance.

He pulled into a filling station at the edge of town.

"Jeez, Mister!" exclaimed the operator, coming forward. "What happened to your tires?"

"Rattlesnakes bit them," Lash retorted. "Put some new ones on, will you? I'm in a hurry."

"Sure. What kind'll you have? The Excello or — "

"Any goddam kind," Lash snapped. "But hurry up!"

The man jacked up the car. He took off one wheel and walked around to the other side. Lash grabbed the tool from his hand. "Put the other one on, while I take this one off."

It took thirty minutes to change the two tires; then another five minutes was wasted paying for the tires and convincing the man that the tire rims didn't need tinkering.

Ready, finally, he looked at his watch. It was exactly fifty-five minutes since the girl had shot out his tires. She had been six miles out on the graveled road. Estimating that she would head for Highway 66 again, that she couldn't average better than a mile a minute on the graveled road, she was probably just now turning onto 66.

His road was thirty miles shorter than the one she had traveled. So she had approximately that much head start on him. It wasn't too much. Exactly 60 miles to the New Mexico line. For Lash. For the girl, 130 miles.

Her top speed on the straight plateau

road was around seventy-five miles per hour, a mile or two over, perhaps. Certainly less than eighty. Lash could do ninety-five. Perhaps . . . more. In an hour he could gain twenty miles on her. In two hours, forty miles. Yes, he ought to catch her somewhere between the Painted Desert and the New Mexico line.

He shot out of Flagstaff, raced beside the highest peak in Arizona — San Francisco Peak — and flashed into the extensive Coconino National Forest, where his headlights made a tunnel between the dwarfed pine trees.

It was downhill now and after the first dozen miles out of Flagstaff, the road was as straight as a surveying instrument could make it.

For the first time, then, since he had owned it, Lash let the car with the stepped-up motor out to its limit. The needle went up to ninety-five, hesitated not at all and eased up to one hundred. It began vibrating then and Lash knew if a tire blew out it wouldn't even be worth while for anyone to pick up the pieces. But he gave the gas pedal the last bit of pressure it would take. The needle went up to 105, quivered and moved up a little more. At 108 it stopped.

Lash held it there until he saw a curve far ahead, then eased off. On the next straightaway he let it out again.

It was fifty-five miles from Flagstaff to Winslow. Lash probably broke every standing record for that trip. It was four A.M. now; there wasn't another car on the road and he simply held his coupé in the center and gave it all.

The gray dawn was breaking in the east when he scudded into Winslow and swished into a gas station.

"Did a girl driving a car with a California license pass here in the last hour?" he cried to the filling station attendant.

The man blinked sleepily. "Dunno, been takin' a nap. Want some gas?"

Lash did not even reply. He shot out of the gas station and hurtled through the village, at three times its posted speed limit. It was thirty-five miles, then, to the mining town of Holbrook. He made it in twenty-six minutes. The road was not too good.

Here for a moment, he was faced with

a problem. He pulled into a gas station, told the man to fill up the tank and studied his map. U.S. Highway 260 slanted off to the south and east. It went ninety-four miles to Springerville, where it met Transcontinental Highway Number 60, that same highway that Lash had shunned back in California.

New Mexico was a sparsely settled state, particularly the southwestern section of it. The roads were too few there. Lash did not believe the girl would venture so far off her regular course. She knew by now that Lash's car was fast, but she couldn't know how fast. She certainly wouldn't count on more than ten miles faster than her own. She was figuring on a minimum of an hour's start — perhaps believed he wouldn't continue the pursuit.

Lash got out money to pay for his gasoline. "I don't suppose you saw a California car with a girl go by here . . . "

"Shore did," was the surprising reply. "'Bout ten minutes ago. Car musta been going seventy. Lucky she didn't wake up our cop, 'cause he'd got her, sure."

Lash threw the surprised man two dollars and without waiting for change, shot out of the station.

It was seventy-three miles to the New Mexico line. Just about an hour's run for her. Lash could do it in forty-five to fifty minutes. At that she was driving faster than he'd expected.

It was twenty miles to the Painted Desert, another twenty to the road that led southward, off the highway, to the Petrified Forest.

The morning gray came grudgingly up the plateau horizon. The headlights of the car were not quite as effective now, but Lash strained his eyes for a glimpse of a red taillight.

It failed to materialize. He held his foot savagely upon the floor boards for forty miles. His motor was roaring and Lash expected any moment that it would explode into a million pieces.

Fifty miles and he dared hold the pace no longer. It was absolute certainty that the girl could not have held her car to its top speed for this long. But where was it?

He drove five or six miles at a moderate seventy, then pressed down once more. Sixty-five miles, daylight, and no car ahead of him. The New Mexico line was only eight miles off now.

He saw the signs pointing to the aboriginal cliff dwellings on the left and groaned. Ahead was the arch that indicated the state line. He rushed under it into New Mexico, made a half turn to the left — and saw a car a half mile ahead.

He overtook it as if it were standing and saw that it was a topless flivver driven by an Indian with a squaw sitting in the middle of the back seat.

It was no use. He'd passed her somewhere between here and Holbrook. She had left the road, probably pulled to the side at the Painted Desert, waited until he'd flashed by and then turned and gone back. She might have taken any one of several crossing graveled roads. The chance of picking up the right one was too slim.

He raised his foot from the gas pedal and coasted along at a slow fifty to the port of entry building outside of Gallup, twenty miles into New Mexico. He stopped for the brief car inspection and questioned the inspector.

The man shook his head. "Only had two cars in the last hour. Both of 'em Reservation Apaches. Gallup is the Indian capital, you know. More Indians here than Whites."

19

LASH drove on into Gallup, through the mile-high city and to the advertised 'World's Biggest Ranch House,' probably the swankiest hotel in the state. He felt like an Indianapolis Speedway racer who has just come in fifth — out of the money, after 500 grueling miles.

He parked his car outside of the 'ranch house' and went into the coffee shop. He ordered ham and eggs and then placed his elbows on the counter and rested his head in his cupped hand, until the waitress brought his order.

He ate without tasting the food, had an extra cup of coffee, then strolled into the Indian curio room. He glanced indifferently over an array of Indian blankets and was about to step outside, when a man he had not noticed spoke to him from the depths of an armchair.

"Driving all night, Mister?"

Lash nodded briefly and would have

gone on, but that the man spoke to him again. "Night driving's bad, Mister. Ought to be a law against it. They brought in a fella here early yesterday morning. Pretty badly cut up and lucky he was alive. Fell asleep at the wheel, he said. Fella from California, too."

"How do you know I'm from California?" Lash asked idly.

"Saw your car. See them all." The man shook his head. "My trouble's *not* being able to sleep. I've got insomnia."

Lash looked curiously at the man suffering from insomnia, then became suddenly alert. "Maybe you remember a friend of mine who passed through here yesterday? Man about forty-five, well-dressed, looks like a banker — "

"Yeah, sure! Say — that's the man I was telling you about, fella got hurt. Didn't want his real name to get out."

"What?" exclaimed Lash. "How do you know?"

"He signed the register, Oscar Perkins, but registration tag on his steering wheel had another name. Vincent Springer. I looked."

Lash inhaled softly. "You say he signed

the register here? You mean he's *staying* here? . . . "

"Not now. The doc put a couple of stitches in his head, eased the kink out of a couple of ligaments, and told him to rest in bed a day. He checked out yesterday evening. Still pretty wobbly . . . "

"Thanks," snapped Lash, heading for the door at the far end of the curio room.

He stepped into the room that constituted the lobby. A sleepy-eyed clerk looked at him over a desk.

"Good morning, sir. What can I do? . . . "

"The man who was brought in here yesterday morning, injured — Oscar Perkins — can you tell me if his car was badly injured?"

"Why, yes, it seemed to be. I know Mr. Perkins was considerably wrought up because it took them so long to repair it. He checked out the moment it was finished . . . "

"What garage worked on it?"

"The official ranch garage, the Navajo Garage . . . "

"Where is it?"

"Why, it's two blocks up the street, in town."

Lash strode out of the hotel, got into his car and drove back to the Navajo Garage.

A man was dozing in the garage office, chair tilted back, feet up on a scarred desk. He blinked when Lash came slamming into the office.

"Want your car, Mister?"

"I haven't got one here. But I want to ask about the California car that you repaired yesterday, the one cracked up in an accident."

"Uh, sure. What about it?"

"How badly was it damaged?"

"Seventy-two dollars' worth. An axle was bent, the cylinder head damaged, the wheels — "

"Never mind the details," Lash said crisply. "What make of car was it? And did you keep a record of the license number?"

"Sure, but — but why d'you wanta know?"

"Insurance company."

"Oh!" The garage man pulled out a card file, skimmed over some cards

273

and stopped at one. "Yeah, here it is. Thirty-eight LaSalle. License 6 W 26-12. Registration, Vincent Springer. That's funny; the man who paid the bill called himself Oscar Perkins. Guess he works for Springer."

"Thanks," said Lash, walking out of the garage.

He drove back to the hotel and questioned the clerk once more "This man, Oscar Perkins, did he make any telephone calls while he stayed here?"

The clerk consulted his records. "I have him down for two long-distance calls; one to Pasadena, California, and the other — mm — to Mesa, New Mexico."

"What numbers at those places?" Lash asked, poised like a cat about to pounce upon a mouse.

"Not given," was the laconic answer.

Lash groaned. The mouse had eluded his grasp and ducked into its hole.

He picked up the telephone from the desk, said into it, "Give me the long-distance operator." Then, "This is Simon Lash, of the Federal Bureau of Investigation. I'm calling from the Gallup

Rancho. A man who was a guest here yesterday made two long-distance calls, one to Pasadena, California, the other to Mesa, New Mexico. I want the numbers he called at those places . . . What?" Lash looked at the clerk, who was regarding him, wide-eyed.

"She wants you to identify me." Lash thrust the phone at the clerk.

The latter nodded, said: "It's all right. This is Albert Norton talking."

Lash pulled the phone back. "Give me that information right away."

It came after a moment. "In Pasadena, the number was Alcazar 7589. In Mesa, 2629. Both were station-to-station calls."

"Thank you," Lash said. "Keep this confidential."

He hung up and looked about the lobby until he saw a telephone booth. "Give me a stack of quarters," he said to the clerk, "I want to make a long-distance call of my own."

He gave the man a five-dollar bill and received a handful of quarters in return.

Entering the booth, he called his apartment in Hollywood. Eddie Slocum answered sleepily, but his tone quickened

275

when he recognized Lash's voice.

"Where you at, Chief?"

"Gallup, New Mexico. And I haven't got much time. I've been chasing Drusilla Denham all night and I just lost her a little while ago . . . "

"That's nothing," Eddie cut in. "The cops lost her yesterday . . . "

"Because they're dopes!" Lash snapped. "They became color blind. A platinum blonde buys a brand new yellow Packard and the cops think this is a cinch. They don't stop to think that's exactly what the girl wants them to think. While they're looking for that yellow car, she gets a six-year-old Chrysler, dyes her hair dark-brown and gives them the slip, down the side roads. They'll probably find the yellow car — in a few days. But they won't find Drusilla. But the hell with that. Here's what I want you to do. Find out who has Telephone Number Alcazar 7589, in Pasadena. A man named Vincent Springer called that number from here, yesterday . . . "

"Springer?" yelped Eddie. "Is he out there, too?"

"Of course! Do you think I chased

Drusilla just for the exercise? She's meeting him somewhere. Here's another job. Auto license 6 W 26-12. Check on the registration. Now, what's the situation in town?"

"Not so good. Sheriff Rucker called. Says Leon Welker's disappeared into thin air. Also he got the local cops looking for Oscar Loomis. He's missing, too. And, of course, they didn't find Drusilla at Palm Springs, where she was supposed to have gone the other day. She'd never even checked in there . . . "

"I know that. What about Joyce Bonniwell? Have you checked up on her?"

"No, but I got Otis to put a man on her house. He called in at ten o'clock last night to say she'd gone to bed."

"How'd he know? Did he peek into her window?"

Eddie chuckled. "He probably did . . . How's the car, Chief?"

"Too light. It would hold the road better with five hundred pounds added. But . . . it does 108 . . . "

"A hundred and eight!" cried Eddie. "Jeez, you actually let her out?"

"Of course! Now, get that information as soon as you can and telephone the operator at Mesa, New Mexico. Tell her I'll stop in as soon as I get there. And stick close to the phone, today. I may wash this up . . . if I'm lucky."

He hung up and leaving the Gallup Rancho, climbed into his car. Study of his road map told him that Mesa was eighty-two miles from Gallup. It was now twenty minutes to seven and he ought to make it nicely by eight o'clock.

He got his gas tank filled at the edge of the town and then started off, driving at a brisk seventy-five-miles an hour. He had seen very little of Arizona, during the night drive, but he saw enough of New Mexico now. He knew vaguely that he was driving at an altitude of from five to six thousand feet, for all this land was plateau country. Here and there was an occasional grade, but the car took them with no perceptible effort.

It was barren, rugged country. Ancient lava rock was strewn in preponderance. In other places, mountains of sandstone seemed to have been dumped willy-nilly by some gigantic prehistoric hand.

It was still early morning but he began to pass cars along the road, mostly dilapidated flivvers driven by stolid Navajo Indians. Strung out beside the highway were tiny adobe sheds, looking from a distance like dwarfed telephone booths, incongruous in their bleak settings. When you came opposite them you generally found them occupied by an Indian woman, who held out brightly coloured pottery or Navajo blankets.

Indian hogans stood in the most impossible surroundings. It was not uncommon to see a field of tremendous boulders and in their very midst a red adobe hogan, with it's inevitable flea-bitten horse, futiley seeking grazing grass. That they found it was apparent by there mere existence, yet Lash would have sworn that there wasn't enough vegetation in a thousand acres of this country to keep alive a mountain goat.

He rolled through the village of Thoreau and at exactly twenty minutes to eight, made a sharp left turn in the road, crossed over the Sante Fé tracks and almost before he saw it, shot into Mesa.

20

MESA seemed to have been dumped right into the middle of the New Mexico desert, yet it was a surprisingly modern little town in many respects. It had several attractive store buildings and neon signs were everywhere. While he was looking for a place to park, Lash saw a sign: "Mesa Hotel."

He rolled the coupé up to the curb and stopped. Climbing out he went into the hotel. A man wearing Levi's, flannel shirt and high-heeled boots, got up from a modern, leather-covered armchair, and went behind the desk. He was an Indian and said in astonishingly precise English:

"Good morning, sir! What can I do for you?"

Lash looked about the lobby, saw no one else around and approached the desk. "I'm looking for a man who arrived in Mesa some time yesterday evening. I don't know what name he's using, but he's driving a LaSalle car, with California license plates, 6 W 26–12."

The Indian said, "You're an FBI man? Mind letting me see your credentials?"

Lash smiled icily. "I'm a private detective. But it's important that I locate that man — quickly."

"Well," said the Indian, "my name is Jeff Spotted Tail. It so happens that I am the town marshal. Any arrests that are made here, I make. It's a fee office, you see."

"I see," Lash said grimly. "And how much do they pay you for arrests?"

"Two dollars and a half."

Lash took out three dollars and laid them on the desk. "Buy yourself a cigar with the change."

"Why, thank you, I will," replied Marshal Jeff Spotted Tail. He moved to the cigar case and brought out a box. Removing one he stuck it into his shirt pocket. Then he tendered the box to Lash. "Will you have one?"

Lash took a cigar, crumpled it in his hand and let the tobacco fall on the floor.

The Indian regarded the proceedings

calmly. "Just who is this man you want to arrest?"

"He used the name of Oscar Perkins in Gallup."

"But that isn't his real name. What is it? Perhaps I've heard it."

"Perhaps you have. But I paid you your fee and I don't see — "

"Ah, but that's just the point! A man has to earn a dollar in whatever manner he can. The town pays me a fee for every arrest I make, but in addition I am permitted to keep whatever reward money a culprit will bring. So you see . . . " Spotted Tail turned up the palms of his swarthy hands and shrugged.

Lash regarded him steadily. "I think I'll play it my own way."

Marshal Spotted Tail let him get almost to the door before he said quietly, "But you cannot make any arrests in my bailiwick."

Lash turned back. "There's no reward offered for this man. I haven't even got a paying client. But I want him — and I'll personally guarantee you $500.00."

Marshal Jeff Spotted Tail tapped a bell on the desk and an Indian boy of about sixteen popped out from behind a Navajo blanket hung on the wall, which evidently concealed a small door.

"Manuel," the marshal-hotel man said, "take over." He reached under the desk and produced a .38 automatic, which he stuck into the waistband of his trousers.

Then he joined Lash. "The man you want calls himself Paul Plennert now."

"He's not even original with his names," Lash remarked. "Where's he holing up?"

"I'll find out in a minute. Nothing happens around here that I don't know about . . . "

"Or get a cut on?" Lash said sarcastically.

The Indian did not seem to mind. "Quite right. I see you're also from Hollywood. I wouldn't be surprised if the man you're seeking is Vincent Springer, the absconding bank president. I imagine, therefore, that you'll be Simon Lash, the eccentric detective . . . "

"Eccentric?"

"That's what the papers call you. As a matter of fact, I was reading about you only this morning. A California sheriff issued a rather bitter statement concerning you. Intimated that you were withholding information from the police."

"I won't withhold any from you," Lash said. "I probably couldn't if I tried. So, where's your telephone office."

"Right over there, opposite that tourist court. I'll introduce you to the local manager."

"That's damn decent of you," Lash retorted. "It'll also give you the opportunity of listening in on what I say."

"Right!"

They entered the little one-story building, but the manager did not seem to be around. Marshal Spotted Tail, however, went straight through the front office into a back room where two operators sat at a switchboard.

"Julia," the marshal said to one of them, "this gentleman wants to ask you some questions."

"The name is Simon Lash. Has a long-distance call come in for me?"

The operator looked at the town marshal. The latter nodded.

"Yes, Mr. Lash," the operator said;

then, "it came in about twenty minutes ago."

"From a Mr. Slocum," Spotted Tail said quietly.

"You *do* own this town," Lash snapped. "All right, can you get Mr. Slocum for me, now?"

The girl plugged in switches, and, after a moment, nodded to a telephone standing near by, on a small desk. Lash walked over and scooped up the phone.

"Lash talking, Eddie. Shoot!"

"It's Springer's car, all right, Chief," Eddie said. "But the Pasadena number was a bust. It's a third-rate hotel in Pasadena. The call was for a Mrs. Zollicker, which was probably our friend under a phony name. Anyway, Mrs. Z. stayed only overnight."

"That's all right, Eddie, I was expecting that. I'm in an interesting situation right now. However, it's well in hand and I'm expecting results today. What about Mrs. B? . . . "

Eddie cleared his throat. "I was afraid you'd ask about her. That Otis op is a dope. He watched the light in her bedroom. It was on until two A.M.,

285

when it was put out. This morning he discovers the garage is empty. Mrs. B. has flown the coop. I'm sorry as hell, Chief. I told Otis what I thought of his operator, but — "

"It's all right, Eddie," Lash said, with surprising mildness. "The Otis man is in character with everyone else that's had anything to do with this affair — just plain stupid! I'll give you a buzz later in the day — I hope. So long!"

He hung up and returned to the switchboard. "Now, then, who has Telephone Number 2629?"

Julia, the operator, looked again at the marshal before replying. "Why, that's the P.C. Ranch. Shall I ring them for you?"

"No, no, Julia," Marshal Spotted Tail cut in. He smiled at Lash. "That's Pete Connors' place. Pete is our local bad man. The ranch is about twenty miles up in the hills."

"Aren't you coming along?"

"Yes. I have no legal authority that far out, but Pete has considerable respect for me, and will co-operate. Shall we use your car, Mr. Lash?"

Lash shrugged and they left the telephone building. After they had climbed into Lash's coupé and he had started the motor, Marshal Spotted Tail revealed his knowledge of automobiles. "A stepped-up motor, eh? Very clever, Lash. How much'll she do?"

"A hundred and eight. Which way?"

"First turn to the right, then when you pass the two-story adobe, look sharp for the road on the left. It's really only a trail."

Actually, it consisted of twin ruts worn into the sand. Once in them, Lash had only to hold the wheel steady. Driving at a modest thirty-five to forty, the wheels held the ruts well enough so Lash could have closed his eyes.

"This Connors," Marshal Spotted Tail remarked after they had driven a couple of miles, "is one of our old-timers. He claims his father was a pal of Billy the Kid's back in the Lincoln County War. Pete thinks he's tougher than his father was. I throw him in jail now and then when he comes to town. I make twenty to thirty dollars a year on him in fees."

"Nice neighbor," Lash said sarcastically.

"I wonder how my man ever connected up with him?"

"'Birds of a feather,' you know," the educated Indian quoted. "I forgot to tell you that there might be some fireworks."

Lash reached over and opened the glove compartment. He took out the gun and dropped it into his right-hand coat pocket. Spotted Tail nodded approvingly.

"That's the place up there."

Lash looked ahead. "Where?"

"Straight ahead and a little to the left."

Lash's eyes followed Spotted Tail's pointing finger and saw a small huddle of adobe buildings. "Thought you said it was twenty miles from town."

Spotted Tail laughed. "We've come about four, now. Those buildings are still sixteen miles away."

"They don't look over a couple of miles."

"This is mesa country, Mr. Lash. The ranch seems to be about halfway up the mountain grade. Would you be surprised to know that peak is forty miles from here?"

"I wouldn't be surprised if it was a

mirage," Lash retorted. "I don't expect much of this country."

"I like it," said the Indian quietly. "My people have lived here — for a thousand years."

"I won't invade your territory. Just give me the man I want and I'll pull out as fast as I came."

The Indian was silent for several miles. Lash, studying the ranch buildings ahead, wished that they did not have to approach so directly. If his quarry spotted him — and if he had the co-operation of Pete Connors, as seemed likely — the situation might prove a little difficult, despite Spotted Tail's apparent confidence.

As they came closer, the ranch buildings increased in size. One, in fact, looked like an ancient citadel, built to withstand Indian attacks.

When they were within a mile of the P.C. Ranch, Lash, disregarding the roughness of the road, gave the coupé the gas. He did not want them at the ranch to have too much time to prepare a reception committee.

Spotted Tail grunted as he was

slammed around beside Lash. "Nice engine you've got on this car. What's the secret of it?"

"Two hundred and fifty dollars," Lash replied. Then, "That man in front of the stockade gate; hasn't he got a rifle in his hands?"

"Oh yes. That's customary. Pete has a telescope. He recognized us fifteen miles back."

Lash slackened speed and coasted up to the man with the rifle. He was dressed in the typical costume of the country, faded Levi's, patched flannel shirt, broad-brimmed hat and high-heeled boots.

"Howdy, Marshal," he greeted Spotted Tail. "Lookin' for somethin'?"

"That's right, the boss. Is he home?"

"Maybe. Who's your friend?"

"A detective from Los Angeles. I believe he has some business with — your guest."

The cowboy had the rifle cradled in his left arm. It was a well-oiled, repeating Winchester, Lash noted.

"What guest?" asked the cowboy. "We ain't got none."

"Why," said Spotted Tail, "in that

case, I'll just say hello to my uncle and run along back to town."

The cowboy scowled, then stepped aside. Lash shifted into low gear and as the cab moved forward through the gate, he shot a sharp glance at the Indian beside him.

"You didn't say you had an uncle out here?"

"Oh," said the Indian. "Did I forget to mention that? Why, Pete Connors is my uncle. I'm half-white, you know."

Lash hadn't known. He brought the car to a stop inside the ranch yard. A tall, bowlegged man of about fifty was coming from the house. A long-barreled revolver was stuck in the waistband of his trousers.

"Hello, Jeff," he said casually.

Spotted Tail nodded. "Hello, Uncle Pete. This is Mr. Simon Lash, a detective from Los Angeles."

Pete Connors showed snaggleteeth in a wicked grin. "Welcome to Robbers Roost, Mr. Detective. Won't you step down and stay awhile?"

Lash dropped his hands into his lap. Instantly Spotted Tail gripped the pocket of his coat and deftly removed Lash's revolver. He tossed it to his uncle, who caught it expertly.

"This is going to cost you money, Uncle Pete," he said.

"I'm not getting much, Jeff," Pete Connors said. "Only a couple of hundred — "

"Then you're being gypped," Spotted Tail said pleasantly. "Your customer absconded with about two hundred thousand. You ought to get fifty of it — "

"But I ain't!" Connors howled. "He says it's a lie. He got only about thirty thousand and he argued like hell about giving me five."

"Is that so?" Spotted Tail said coldly. "Better talk to him some more. My cut's ten thousand, or I don't play."

"A couple of buzzards fighting over a rabbit they didn't even kill," Simon Lash remarked grimly.

Spotted Tail regarded him without expression. "You *are* a rabbit, Lash. You came walking into my place just like one. I'd expected more of you, Simon Lash."

"You haven't seen my hole card yet."

"You haven't got one."

Lash shrugged. "Do we sit here? The sun's getting warm."

Spotted Tail climbed out of the car, on his side. Lash stretched, yawned and got out on his own side. Pete Connors regarded him curiously.

"You sure this is Simon Lash, Jeff?" he asked. "I read a piece about him in a true detective story magazine once. He don't look like much."

"You don't look so good, either," Lash retorted.

"My dad rode with Billy the Kid," Connors said proudly. "And I ain't done so badly on my own. I own most of the country around here and my sister's kid, Jeff here, runs things in Mesa . . . "

"You talk too much, Uncle Pete," Spotted Tail said coldly. "Let's get this over with. I've got some businesses in town, you know. Where's this — guest — of yours?"

"He's bashful," Pete Connors said. "We'll have to go and talk to him."

"Oh, he's at — he isn't here? All right, let's take Mr. Lash's car. He says

293

it'll do a hundred and eight. I don't believe it."

Spotted Tail climbed in behind the wheel of Lash's coupé and his uncle walked around and got in beside him. Without another glance at Lash, Spotted Tail backed the car out of the courtyard, turned it and scooted off.

Lash stared after the car, his forehead creased. They had left him standing here, unguarded. He walked to the gate.

Spotted Tail had left the rutted road leading to Mesa and cut off across country toward the mountain peak, to the right. Lash watched the car bounce over the uneven terrain and wondered idly if the springs would stand the trip. Spotted Tail was driving at at least seventy-five.

He looked around. The man with the rifle, who had accosted him and Spotted Tail as they came up, was lying on the ground near by. The rifle was within his reach, but the man seemed to be paying no attention to Lash.

21

LASH turned and sunlight, reflected, flashed into his eyes. He looked up and saw a small tower over the main house. A man was up there, a rifle barrel stuck out carelessly over a three-foot parapet.

No wonder Connors and Spotted Tail weren't worrying about Lash. The place was a regular fort and there wasn't a shred of cover within miles of the ranch. A man attempting to escape from here could be picked off by the riflemen at their leisure.

Lash said to the man lying on the ground, "Nice place you have here."

"Ain't it?" the man grunted in reply.

"What does your boss do — besides rustling cattle?"

The man sat up, grinning crookedly. "We ain't rustled a steer in fifteen year. You been seein' Western movies, Pardner. Not that I don't like the movies myself. I go every Sunday. I like Gene Autry. Say, I hear you're from Hollywood. Ever see Gene around there?"

"Once or twice."

"Is that so? What's he like?"

"Just like he is on the screen. A nice chap. Personally, I like Donald Duck."

"You do? So do I. Boy, d'you see him in that last one — Officer Duck, where he was going out to pinch some crook called Tiny Tim, who turns out to be a big gorilla? I laughed my head off at that one."

"Ha-ha," said Lash mirthlessly. "What's the setup around here? Is this fellow, Connors, really as tough as he makes out?"

"Tougher, Mister. But the real tough one is that half-breed nephew of his, Spotted Tail."

"I was wondering about him. He's about thirty, isn't he? How'd he ever get to be that old?"

"The boys often talk about that. I was going to knock him off myself, about six months ago."

"Why didn't you?"

"He beat me to the draw. I got fined two bucks for that."

Lash caught the sly look of derision on the man's face and, turning, went back into the ranch courtyard. It was cooler in here. He walked to the porch of the long adobe house, which was covered with red tiles. There were a couple of wicker chairs on it and he sat down in one of them.

He leaned back, closed his eyes, and was asleep almost instantly.

He was awakened by the return of his coupé. He sat in the chair and watched Spotted Tail and his uncle climb out and approach. Neither of the two looked very happy.

"Cheerio!" Lash said. "The city slicker too much for you?"

"He hasn't got the money with him," Spotted Tail said in annoyance.

"You didn't think he'd bring two hundred thousand with him, did you? To a place called Robbers Roost?"

"Oh, that's only our private name for this place," said Peter Connors. "Anyway, Mister, we settled *your* hash."

"Did you now? What is it, the knife or the stake? Of course, Jeff, you haven't forgotten my little phone conversation?"

"No, I didn't," replied Spotted Tail glowering. "Not that your friend could get anywhere. It's just that we don't like outsiders prowling around here."

"So? . . . "

"So you'll stay here as a guest until — well, until the other guest can clear up his affairs."

"And make a getaway, you mean? In other words, he's waiting here for his girl friend?"

"What do you know about a girl friend?"

"Oh, hasn't she telephoned yet? I thought she might have. She was delayed in Arizona."

Spotted Tail looked at his uncle and the latter squinted. "Maybe he'd like to know about that . . . "

"No," said Spotted Tail quickly. He signaled by a jerk of his head and his uncle followed him to one side of the courtyard. Lash watched them whispering for a few minutes and chuckled.

When they came back, Spotted Tail said, "Did you really see the woman?"

"That depends. What's her name?"

Spotted Tail scowled. "I hate a wise

guy. All right, Uncle Pete, you keep him here. I've got to get back to Mesa. Better have one of the boys drive me back. I'd just as soon not have his car seen around town. Keep it inside."

Peter Connors yelled: "Hey, Luke!" and a man came out of an adobe shed across the courtyard.

Connors said: "Come in the house, Lash."

Lash followed him into the comparative coolness of the adobe ranch house. He was surprised at the luxurious furnishings and mused that outlawry must be profitable in New Mexico. Navajo blankets were everywhere, on the floor, on the walls and draped over cool-looking wicker furniture.

"Sit down," Connors said, gesturing.

Lash seated himself in a blanket-covered armchair. Connors took a turn about the room and finally threw himself on a couch. Lying on his side, facing Lash, he said:

"You offered Jeff five hundred, Lash. How much money can you really raise?"

"At a forced sale? About six hundred. Why?"

"Because our guest is — uh, somewhat unreasonable. We can't get him over five thousand, no matter what."

"Five thousand is pretty good money. What do you give him for that?"

"Haven't you got the layout? That's my business. Fellas like to take a vacation — a quiet vacation — home here and stay until it's safe."

"Until the heat is off? I get it, Connors. The law's fixed and even if it wasn't — you can see them coming a long way off."

"That's right. There's a nice back door over the peak. The other side's plenty rough . . . and my boys know the trails. We ain't never lost a guest yet. How'd you happen to get as far as Mesa, Lash? I was listening on the radio around breakfast time and the police over in California didn't seem to have much idea about — things."

Lash shrugged. "I sort of walked into it, didn't I? I've had bad breaks all along. Otherwise, I'd had him two days ago."

Connors frowned. "Jeff underrates people. He's so danged conceited himself. He shouldn't have let you make that telephone call in town. Say, I wonder . . . "

"Yes?"

"Why, I was just thinkin' maybe, since you were so close behind, if you didn't maybe know where he stached that two hundred thousand? I could make you an interesting proposition . . . "

"I haven't paid much attention to that end of it," said Lash. "But if I could talk to your man . . . "

"No, that's out. He absolutely says no."

"How come? Does he think his identity is a secret?"

"Dunno. Last thing he said, was he'd light out if I brought anyone else up to see him. And since I haven't got my money . . . "

A muffled telephone rang somewhere in the room. Connors sat up and hit the rounded end of the sofa. It sprang up and Lash saw that it was hinged. Connors reached into the hollow and brought out a handset telephone.

"Hello," he said. "Pete Connors . . . Yeah . . . Uh-huh . . . Everything's okay . . . Fine . . . "

He put the receiver back on the prongs,

scowled at Lash, then reached in and pulled out the entire phone cord, which had a plug at the end of it.

"Just in case," he said. "Excuse me." He walked out of the room, returning in a moment without the telephone.

"Nice," said Lash. "You think of everything."

"That's why I'm still in business. I guess you won't be here so long, after all. That was his friend. She's comin' out, from Mesa. I hope . . . "

"That she's got the money with her? Two to one she hasn't."

"You're not a very cheerful guy, Lash," Connors scowled. "It's tough enough making a living these days."

A man pounded down concrete stairs and came into the room. He was unshaven, as sunburned as an Apache, and carried a rifle.

"Car comin' from Mesa," he said laconically.

"That's right," Connors replied. "Should be a woman in it. California license plates. Let me know before she comes in."

The rifleman went out again. Lash

heard him climbing the stairs and guessed that the living room was directly under the watchtower.

The boss of the P.C. Ranch said to Lash, "Better come along now."

Lash followed him out of the big living room, down a corridor and into a ten-by-ten room. There was only one window in it and that had iron bars set in the wall. The wall, Lash noted, was more than a foot thick.

There was an army cot in the room, a blanket-draped rocking chair and a shelf of books along one wall. "What's this?" Lash asked. "The dungeon?"

"Uh-huh," Pete Connors replied. "But it's comfortable. You'll get your grub regular and a couple of days in here won't hurt you none."

"Hurt me, hell! I'm that far behind in my sleep." Lash crossed the little room and plopped himself down on the cot. He grinned at the rancher.

Connors chuckled. "I like a man who plays them as they come. I'll look in later."

He closed the door and Lash heard a bar fall in place outside. He rose quickly from the cot and went to the door. He tapped it lightly with his finger and whistled softly. It was made of two-inch planking. It would take a battering ram to break it down.

He went to the window and saw nothing but bleak desert land. The window opened on a dead side. He could see neither the road approaching the ranch nor the trail leading up into the mountains. Which was probably the intent of the architect who had planned this room.

A frown creased his forehead. He had made glib conversation with Pete Connors and his scoundrelly nephew, Spotted Tail, but he was in a far from flippant mood.

He'd lost the game. Eddie Slocum would worry when he didn't hear from him again, and along toward evening, or the next morning, he might even telephone to Mesa. In which case Jeff Spotted Tail would promptly learn of it. It would be another day, then, perhaps two, before Eddie would come looking for Lash. By that time it would be too late. If Eddie, by any chance, came to

Mesa sooner, he would step into the same trap into which Lash had walked so blindly.

Lash cursed silently. He'd had victory in the palm of his hand and the palm had turned over and the knuckles came up and slapped him in the teeth.

He walked back to the cot and threw himself down on it. But he couldn't sleep. After awhile he rolled over and glanced at the titles of the books in the shelf, which was right beside the cot.

He came up to a sitting position, gasping. His hand shot out and caught down a volume at random. The title of it was *Wolfville Nights* and while it was somewhat dusty it was in excellent condition, having probably been read only two or three times.

Quickly he put the book down on the cot and whipped another from the shelf; *Clay Allison of the Washita*.

"Thirty-five dollars or I'll eat it," he muttered.

The third book he took from the shelf was *The Book of Mormon*, a rather bulky volume. He looked at the flyleaf and perspiration broke out upon his forehead.

He leaned back a moment, staring at the shelf, then drawing a deep breath, reached to the far end where there were a number of thinner books and pamphlets. He took down a stack of them, ran over them quickly. The next to the last one of the lot was a pamphlet of twenty-four pages with the lengthy title:

THE LATTER DAY SAINTS' EMIGRANTS' GUIDE, Being a Table of Distances Showing All the Springs, Creeks, Rivers, Hills, Mountains, Camping Places and All Other Notable Places, from Council Bluffs, to the Valley of the Great Salt Lake.

"It's not true," Lash whispered. "This couldn't happen to me — not now!"

He was so engrossed in his examination of the books that he did not hear the bar on the outside of his door being raised. The first he was aware of it, Pete Connors was pushing open the door.

"Hello," he said, "what're you doin'?"

"Looking over your books," Lash said,

making a strenuous effort to sound matter-of-fact. "You're quite a reader."

"Me? Uh-huh. I ain't read a book since I was twelve years old. I go for the true detective magazines, that's about all. My old man was a great reader. Them was his books."

"The fellow who rode with Billy the Kid?"

"Sure, how many fathers did you think I had."

"I don't know," Lash replied dryly. "There are some Mormon books here . . . "

"They don't mean nothin'. My old man was quite a lad, in his time. He joined the Mormon Church once when he was shinin' up to a Mormon gal. Used to be quite a few Mormons around here. Still are, on the other side of the mountain. But say, ain't you interested in the gal who was just here? She's a peach."

"You told her about me?"

"Yeah, sure. She got kinda excited. Wanted to see her boy friend right away. One of the boys took her up to him."

"What about the money? Did she have it with her?"

"Nah, just a couple of thousand. But don't worry, they ain't gonna get away from here without payin' off."

"That's right," said Lash. "Make them pay. They've killed three people between them. One of them was a girl."

"I ain't interested in what the guests did before they came here," Pete Connors said hastily. "I run a quiet business, just like my dad did before me. Would you believe that Billy the Kid stayed here for a month? That was just before he left for Fort Summer, where Pat Garrett got him. Lots of other famous men stopped here in their time. Johnny Ringo — Dad said Johnny was a great reader, too — Dave Rudabaugh, Butch Cassidy . . . this was a post-office for the Wild Bunch at the time. We never asked no questions about anyone, when they was here. As long as they paid, we gave them good service."

"You ought to write a book," Lash said.

Connors grinned. "We've had writin' fellas here as guests. They was on the dodge, too."

A man came up the corridor and rapped on the open door with the barrel of a revolver. "There's a telephone call, Pete, and I can't find the telephone."

"I hid it," said Connors. "Excuse me." He backed out of the room and Lash heard the bar fall into place again. He sprang up from the cot, then, and made a quick search of the room.

Aside from the books, the chair and the cot, there were no other movable objects of any weight that could be used as a weapon. He studied the bed for a moment, then shook his head.

He tested the rocking chair and knew that he could break it. But the breakage would probably be noticed instantly by anyone coming into the room.

As he moved around, his hand brushed his trousers pocket and coins jingled. He thrust his hand into the pocket and brought out a handful of silver, seven or eight dollars, three half dollars and a dozen or so quarters and dimes, left over from playing the slot machine at Williams, Arizona.

He weighed the coins and suddenly his eyes widened. Sitting down on the bed, he quickly removed one shoe and sock. There was a small hole in the toe of the sock, but not large enough to permit the passage of a dime.

He dropped the entire handful of coins into the sock, put a knot in it just above the lump and swung the bludgeon by the loose end of the sock. It smacked into his other hand with a satisfying 'whack.'

He put his shoe back on his bare foot, laced it and stood up. Standing, he could not see his bare ankles and he nodded in satisfaction. He dropped the blackjack into his coat pocket and sat down in the rocking chair to read *The Latter Day Saints' Emigrants' Guide*.

22

IT was a half hour before he heard shoes scrape out in the corridor. He put the book down quickly and rose, so his bare ankles would not show.

It was Connors again, a dejected, worried-looking Pete Connors.

"I've got some bad news for you, Lash," he said. "Very bad."

"What? . . . No supper?"

Connors did not even grin at the joke. He shook his head. "Better come out and talk it over."

Lash shrugged. He followed Connors down the long, cool hall into the blanket-draped living room.

Joyce Bonniwell sat on the couch.

"Hello, Joyce," Lash said.

She stared at him. "You're not surprised?"

"Of course not. I knew it was you."

"You didn't! Not . . . "

"Well, I wasn't sure until you came into the restaurant in Williams."

"But you didn't see my face there!" she cried. "I had the scarf — and I sat with my back to the windows."

"Sure, but you passed me coming in. I didn't see your face, but I recognized — your perfume. You should have changed it."

She leaned forward, staring at him, intently. "What else do you know, Simon?"

"Everything, Joyce. The Drusilla stuff was a little hard to swallow. I don't know for sure if there is a Drusilla Denham, but if there is, the real one's probably in Europe."

"Honolulu," Joyce Bonniwell said. "Go on, why didn't you fall for — Drusilla?"

"It was too pat. She comes up to Ocelot Springs, with Bonniwell. Shows herself openly at the hotel and she's got platinum blond hair, so everyone'll be sure to remember her. Then she disappears. She drives off with Bonniwell's car, but what does she do with it? Take it out into the desert and lose it, or run it off a cliff? Uh-uh. She drives it to Barstow, leaves it on a street and catches a bus to Pasadena. There she buys a brand-new yellow Packard — to match her platinum hair. The cops begin running in circles; they figure it's a cinch to spot such a combination, a good-looking platinum blonde in a yellow Packard. But they don't find either. Because Drusilla takes off her wig and becomes a brunette and the yellow Packard's stored in a private garage — that you probably rented a week before. So you take a taxi back to Hollywood, where you arrive just in time to take Sheriff Rucker's call from Ocelot Springs."

Her blue eyes were slightly tinged with yellow, now. "You figured it all out, didn't you, Simon? I underestimated you."

"No, you overestimated me. You thought I'd be smart enough to smell out all the false trails and bark as I went down each one. You figured that would bring all the bloodhounds down those trails and leave you alone on the main, obvious trail — the Sheridan National Bank. I was too dumb to run down those clever trails. All I could see was that if a man works in a bank and there's monkey business he's robbing the bank . . . At that you almost fooled me a couple of times. You put on a couple of pretty good acts."

Joyce leaned forward, her body taut. "You know that you know too much, Simon? Too much to . . . live?"

Lash shrugged. "Four isn't any worse than three, is it, Joyce? But you know you're finished, don't you?"

"No, I don't know anything of the kind. You're the last — link. We'll catch a plane at Albuquerque tonight. Tomorrow we'll board the Pan-American Clipper at New Orleans. And that's the end of the trail."

"You're forgetting Pete here, Joyce?"

She shook her head. "No, Pete's safe. He's getting twenty-five thousand for this . . . "

"Ah," said Lash, "the ante's gone up." He looked sharply at Pete Connors. There was an unhappy expression on the rancher's face.

"That's a lot of money, Lash. Business hasn't been too good the last couple of years."

"Sure, I know, Pete, but this is one job you can't clean up afterwards. My assistant in Hollywood knows where I am . . . "

"Jeff mentioned that," said Connors, "but he says he can handle that end of it. I'm sorry, Lash . . . "

A harsh voice called from outside the house. "Come on, Joyce, we haven't got all day . . . "

"Your master's voice," said Lash. "Your lord and master."

Joyce came to her feet in a single bound. "What do you mean?" she cried.

Lash chuckled. "Surely you didn't think I believed it was . . . Vincent Springer?"

The color left her face and her mouth fell slightly open. "What . . . who? . . . "

"Why, your husband, of course. Jim Bonniwell . . . "

Lash laughed and dropped his hand into his coat pocket. As he brought it out, he turned. Pete Connors was leaning forward, jaw hanging slack.

Lash swung the coin-weighted sock. He put everything he had into the blow and the sock struck Connors so hard that it burst and coins scattered all over the floor.

Connors' knees buckled and Lash stepping in, caught him. He held him up long enough to whisk the long-barreled revolver from his belt, then let him slump to the floor.

All this took but a second, yet as Lash turned on Joyce Bonniwell, she already had her leather purse open and was bringing out a small revolver.

Lash leaped toward her, swung at her wrist with Pete Connors' revolver and her face with his free, open hand. The blow on her wrist smashed the gun from her hand and his open palm knocked her back to the couch.

She screamed, a combination of pain, hate and just plain — savagery.

She bounced up from the couch and came at Lash, long nails streaking for his face. "Jim! . . . " she cried. "Jim . . . hurry! . . . "

Lash side-stepped and jammed the revolver into her side. "Stop it," he said in cold fury. "Stop it, or so help me, I'll — "

He didn't say it, but she knew. She knew that it was his life or hers . . . and that she had lost any power over him that she might once have had.

He caught her roughly by the shoulder and propelled her toward the hall. Boots were pounding on the veranda and an unshaven, wild-eyed man sprang into the doorway.

"Jim! . . . " Joyce sobbed hysterically.

Thunder exploded in the hallway and a red-hot iron seared along Lash's upper biceps. He shoved Joyce in front of him as a shield, reached under her arm with Connors' revolver and fired at Jim Bonniwell. The bullet clipped off an edge of the adobe doorjamb and Bonniwell sprang back, out of sight.

To the left was a flight of concrete stairs, leading upwards. As Lash pushed Joyce toward them, a door opened at the top of the stairs and a rifle was thrust down. Lash snapped a quick shot up, heard a yell of pain and the rifle came falling down the stairs.

He scooped it up before it landed on the floor, gave Joyce another shove up the stairs and crowded up behind her.

As his head came up into the tower, Lash saw the guard crouching on the floor, holding a bleeding shoulder. Lash gestured him down and the man departed with alacrity. There was a stout trap door that Lash picked up and let fall into place.

He looked around. The tower was about ten feet square, with a roof overhead and an adobe parapet, eighteen inches thick and four feet high. There were slots in it, so a man could fire without exposing himself above the top of the parapet. Lash crouched low and looked at Joyce Bonniwell.

She was standing on the other side, as far from him as she could get. Her face was white, her eyes wide in terror . . . and awe.

A bullet ripped through the trap door. Lash laughed and moved aside. The floor was concrete.

"Cozy," he said to Joyce Bonniwell. "We can't go down, but they can't come up."

She was crouching down now, her body leaning forward, her hand behind her back. Suddenly Lash exclaimed and rushed toward her. Her hands came out from behind her back then, and she clawed his face. Stung, he slapped her savagely and she scuttled on hands and knees for the other side of the parapet.

Then Lash saw what she had been doing. She had been concealing a telephone with her back and had been twisting the wires in an attempt to break them. "Why, goddam you! . . . " he snarled. "I've a good notion to . . . " He thrust the revolver he had taken from Connors to put it into his belt and she, mistaking the first part of the movement, recoiled.

He grinned then and laying the rifle beside him, took the receiver off the hook. He put it to his ear, held his breath for an instant, then let it out, in relief. The wire was live.

The Mesa operator's voice said in his ear: "Number, please."

"I'm calling for Pete Connors," Lash said. "Give me long distance, please."

He heard the click of a connection and a different voice, saying, "Long Distance."

"I want Hollywood, California," Lash said. He gave his own telephone number.

And then while he waited for the connection to be made, he watched Joyce

Bonniwell. She was huddled against the parapet, but her body was still tensed. He guessed that she was debating her chances of making a fight of it long enough, at least, to allow Jim Bonniwell, or one of Connors' men to come up from below.

Lash picked up the rifle with his free hand. He held it carelessly so the muzzle missed Joyce by about a foot. He pulled the trigger.

The bullet smashed into the adobe, sending a shower of splinters over Joyce. She cried out and threw herself flat on the floor.

Lash chuckled and at that moment Eddie Slocum's voice said: "Hello, Chief?"

"Yes," Lash said. "Now, listen, quick. I'm in a jam. I'm holding off a bunch of cutthroats at the Pete Connors' Ranch, twenty miles from Mesa, New Mexico. You can't appeal to the Mesa law, because they're in on it. Telephone Gallup, the state police. I can hold out an hour or two — I hope. I've got Jim Bonniwell here. Yes, of course, he's the — "

He stopped. He had spoken the last

sentence into a dead wire. Either the Mesa operator had been listening in and cut him off, or someone below had cut the wire.

He dropped the telephone.

"Well, Joyce," he said, "this does it. Here we are, all alone, on top of a stack of dyna — " He broke off as another bullet tore through the trap door, then finished, "a stack of dynamite."

Jim Bonniwell's voice came from below, muffled, but recognizably furious. "All right, Lash, I'll make a deal. Send Joyce down and you can stay up there. We'll pull out . . . "

"Where to, Bonniwell?" Lash called back mockingly.

"That doesn't concern you," Bonniwell retorted. "I'm paying Connors, anyway, and he won't touch you. It's your only chance. If I wasn't in a hurry, I wouldn't — "

"*I'm* not in a hurry, Bonniwell. I've just made a telephone call and there'll be a bunch of state troopers here inside of an hour . . . "

Lash heard a rumble of voices below. Evidently Bonniwell was talking it over with someone. Then Pete Connors' voice came through the trap door. "I know you made that phone call, Lash, but the police can't come in time. Anyway, Jeff Spotted Tail will head them off . . . "

"Maybe," said Lash, "and maybe not. I'll play it this way . . . "

"The hell you will, Lash!" roared Bonniwell's voice. "You can't get away. I'll dynamite the tower . . . "

"I was just talking about dynamite. Wasn't I, Joyce?"

Joyce called down. "Careful, Jim. He's . . . desperate."

"So're you," Lash retorted. "And I don't value my life as much as you do . . . You're licked, Bonniwell."

There was more mumbling down below, then silence. Lash looked at Joyce Bonniwell. "Nice fellow, this husband of yours."

Her lips curled. "You never did forgive — or forget. I saw it the first time I went into your office. You were jealous . . . all these years, you were burning with jealousy. Because I threw you over, ten years ago . . . "

Lash chuckled. "Get it out of your

system, Joyce. Go ahead. I don't mind at all . . . not now."

"The hell you don't, Simon Lash. You're as much in love with me today as you were ten years ago. Men don't forget me. Look how I held Jim Bonniwell? Yes, you thought I hadn't been able to hold him. But you found out different. That redhead wasn't Jim's . . . you learned that yourself."

"I did, Joyce. I found out a lot of things. That Bonniwell was just a cheap, small-time crook. He robbed his friends at the club, he double-crossed Vincent Springer, and then when Springer began to close in on him, he lured him up to that mink ranch and killed him. By the way — did you know that I knew *then* that it was Jim Bonniwell I wanted — and no one else? Yeah. The two shots. The first blast didn't quite destroy all of Springer's features, so Bonniwell had to give him another. A messy job. You did a neater one on that poor kid, Evelyn Price . . . "

"I didn't do that!" Joyce cried suddenly. "I didn't kill her. Or anyone . . . " She leaned forward suddenly. "Believe me,

Simon. I — I was only trying to help my husband. He'd gotten in and — "

"Shut up!" Lash snarled suddenly. He cocked his head to one side. Yes, an automobile motor was roaring in the courtyard. Joyce had been trying to drown it out, so Lash wouldn't hear.

Lash put his face to one of the slots in the parapet. He held his eye to the hole for a moment and then a car shot into view. It was heading down the road, leading to Mesa.

Lash drew away from the slot. "Bonniwell's pulling out," he announced. "He's leaving you to take it . . . alone."

She whirled, pressed her face to a slot. "He can't. He — he isn't running out. He isn't! . . . " Her voice rose to a shriek. "Jim! . . . Don't . . . "

Lash thrust the Winchester rifle into the slot. He took careful aim at a rear tire and squeezed the trigger.

The car bumped out of the road ruts, slewed half-way around and came to a stop in a cloud of dust. Lash waited a moment, until Bonniwell sprang out of the car, then he took careful aim again.

Joyce screamed, just as he pulled the

trigger. But it didn't deflect Lash's aim. Jim Bonniwell plunged to the sand, thrashed for a moment, and crawled to a sitting position. His left leg hung limp.

Lash pulled the rifle out of the slot and looked at Joyce Bonniwell. She was staring at him, tears streaking her beautiful face.

"I guess that's that," Lash said.

From down below came Pete Connors' voice. "You got Bonniwell, Lash. There ain't no use us fightin' you. Maybe we can make a deal, Lash."

"Maybe," said Lash, "maybe we can. What's your proposition?"

"I ain't got any. You're a private dick. You can take him — and the girl. As long as you pull out of here and leave me and the boys alone . . ."

"That's a deal, Connors. Step aside, I'm coming down."

He waited a moment, then lifted the trap door and let it fall on its side. Without looking back at Joyce Bonniwell, he descended the stairs. The hall below was empty. So was the courtyard when he stepped out.

He walked carelessly through the gate,

followed the ruts in the sand until he came to within thirty yards of where Jim Bonniwell was sitting in the sand. Then he stopped.

"All right, Bonniwell, let's get it over . . ."

"I can't," Bonniwell gritted. "My gun's in the car. You . . . you've won . . ."

Far down the easy grade, Lash saw a cloud of dust. He studied it for a moment and made out two or three automobiles and smaller black dots that might be motorcycles.

"The police are coming down there, Bonniwell."

"Let 'em come. I'm through. My leg . . . " Pain contorted Jim Bonniwell's face. "You shot me through the kneecap. You've got to get me to a doctor. I can't stand . . ."

"A doctor, Bonniwell? Why, they'll only electrocute you later . . ."

"I know. I can't beat the rap. But now! . . ."

Lash shook his head slowly. "Have you forgotten, Bonniwell? You're dead. You were murdered up in Ocelot Springs, California."

The pain was erased for a moment from Bonniwell's face. He stared at Lash, in astonishment. "What . . . do you mean?"

"Just what I said. Vincent Springer murdered you and absconded with the bank's money. The police of six states are looking for . . . Vincent Springer. It's him they'll send to the death house at San Quentin . . . And the woman who helped him . . . "

"Joyce didn't have anything to do with the killings," Bonniwell capped. "Yeah, she helped me plan the first part of it. But she didn't know there was going to be any killing."

"You killed Springer, Ben Castlemon . . . and Evelyn Price?"

"Of course. Castlemon saw Springer come up to the ranch. And the Price kid — well, I was sorry about her, but she'd seen me with Oscar. She ran into me by bad luck, when I had the room staked out across the street from your apartment . . . "

Lash took Pete Connors' revolver from his belt. There were three live cartridges in the cylinder. He removed two of them, then swung shut the cylinder. He looked down the trail and could make out three automobiles and two motorcycles.

He said: "All right, Bonniwell was murdered at Ocelot Springs. The police are satisfied. They won't bother much if they find Springer took the easy way out . . . when he was cornered." He wet his lips with his tongue and looked down at Bonniwell. "There's one bullet in this gun. Do you understand? . . . "

Bonniwell stared at him for a moment. Then he nodded. "And Joyce?"

"She'll be punished enough, with her husband's insurance already cashed in . . . " He tossed the revolver to Bonniwell, who caught it. Then Lash turned and walked back toward the ranch house.

He had gone twenty feet when the revolver cracked. He did not falter in his step.

Entering the courtyard, he encountered Pete Connors. The latter had his hands up to his shoulders, palms toward Lash.

Lash said: "That man was Vincent Springer. You can tell any story you like how he happened to come here . . . as long as you say his name was Springer. Understand? . . . "

Pete Connors nodded.

★ ★ ★

Lash blew the horn outside the apartment on Harper. Eddie Slocum's face came to the window, then was quickly pulled away. A moment later he was tearing open the front door.

"Chief!" he cried, as he bounded across the sidewalk. "I been waitin' for you . . . "

"Thanks," said Lash sarcastically. "You should have put a lamp in the window. There're some packages in the back. Help me get them in the — house."

There were three packages. Lash carried one himself, and Eddie brought the other two. As he entered the library, Eddie tripped on the rug and one of the packages fell to the floor. The paper binding burst and books scattered to the floor.

"Books!" Eddie cried. "Jeez, Chief, you didn't? . . . "

"I didn't buy them? The hell I didn't, Eddie."

Eddie Slocum staggered back. "But, Chief, you couldn't of. You said over the phone that you weren't getting a fee out of the case. Did you forget that we were broke?"

"No, I didn't forget that. I figure on selling some of these books, at a profit. I got them at a bargain." He grinned. "The guy who owned them couldn't read, anyway, so when I offered him ten dollars for the lot . . ."

"Only ten bucks?" Eddie cried, in relief.

"Uh-uh. And there happens to be included in that lot one of the rarest books in America. The famous *Emigrants' Guide*. I called it to Connors' attention, asked him if he wanted to throw it in with the lot. He said, yes . . ."

Eddie regarded Lash in awe. "But Chief, ain't that *Emigrants' Guide* worth — "

"Does Eisenschiml give *me* what a book's worth? Of course he doesn't. That's the secret of the rare-book business. Buy for as little as you can, sell for as much as you can. That

Emigrants' Guide, figuring it pro rata, cost me fourteen cents ... Umm, the last time I saw it listed, it was offered for twelve hundred ... "

THE END

TO FIGHT THE WILD
Rod Ansell and Rachel Percy

Lost in uncharted Australian bush, Rod Ansell survived by hunting and trapping wild animals, improvising shelter and using all the bushman's skills he knew.

COROMANDEL
Pat Barr

India in the 1830s is a hot, uncomfortable place, where the East India Company still rules. Amelia and her new husband find themselves caught up in the animosities which seethe between the old order and the new.

THE SMALL PARTY
Lillian Beckwith

A frightening journey to safety begins for Ruth and her small party as their island is caught up in the dangers of armed insurrection.

DEATH TRAIN
Robert Byrne

The tale of a freight train out of control and leaking a paralytic nerve gas that turns America's West into a scene of chemical catastrophe in which whole towns are rendered helpless.

THE ADVENTURE OF THE CHRISTMAS PUDDING
Agatha Christie

In the introduction to this short story collection the author wrote "This book of Christmas fare may be described as 'The Chef's Selection'. I am the Chef!"

RETURN TO BALANDRA
Grace Driver

Returning to her Caribbean island home, Suzanne looks forward to being with her parents again, but most of all she longs to see Wim van Branden, a coffee planter she has known all her life.

NURSE ALICE IN LOVE
Theresa Charles

Accepting the post of nurse to little Fernie Sherrod, Alice Everton could not guess at the romance, suspense and danger which lay ahead at the Sherrod's isolated estate.

POIROT INVESTIGATES
Agatha Christie

Two things bind these eleven stories together — the brilliance and uncanny skill of the diminutive Belgian detective, and the stupidity of his Watson-like partner, Captain Hastings.

LET LOOSE THE TIGERS
Josephine Cox

Queenie promised to find the long-lost son of the frail, elderly murderess, Hannah Jason. But her enquiries threatened to unlock the cage where crucial secrets had long been held captive.

THE LISTERDALE MYSTERY
Agatha Christie

Twelve short stories ranging from the light-hearted to the macabre, diverse mysteries ingeniously and plausibly contrived and convincingly unravelled.

TO BE LOVED
Lynne Collins

Andrew married the woman he had always loved despite the knowledge that Sarah married him for reasons of her own. So much heartache could have been avoided if only he had known how vital it was to be loved.

ACCUSED NURSE
Jane Converse

Paula found herself accused of a crime which could cost her her job, her nurse's reputation, and even the man she loved, unless the truth came to light.

DEAD SPIT
Janet Edmonds

Government vet Linus Rintoul attempts to solve a mystery which plunges him into the esoteric world of pedigree dogs, murder and terrorism, and Crufts Dog Show proves to be far more exciting than he had bargained for . . .

A BARROW IN THE BROADWAY
Pamela Evans

Adopted by the Gordillo family, Rosie Goodson watched their business grow from a street barrow to a chain of supermarkets. But passion, bitterness and her unhappy marriage aliented her from them.

THE GOLD AND THE DROSS
Eleanor Farnes

Lorna found it hard to make ends meet for herself and her mother and then by chance she met two men — one a famous author and one a rich banker. But could she really expect to be happy with either man?

IN PALE BATTALIONS
Robert Goddard

Leonora Galloway has waited all her life to learn the truth about her father, slain on the Somme before she was born, the truth about the death of her mother and the mystery of an unsolved wartime murder.

A DREAM FOR TOMORROW
Grace Goodwin

In her new position as resident nurse at Coombe Magna, Karen Stevens has to bear the emnity of the beautiful Lisa, secretary to the doctor-on-call.

AFTER EMMA
Sheila Hocken

Following the author's previous auto-biographies — EMMA & I, and EMMA & Co., she relates more of the hilarious (and sometimes despairing) antics of her guide dogs.

PREJUDICED WITNESS
Dilys Gater

Fleur Rowley finds when she leaves London for her 'author's retreat' in the wilds of North Wales that she is drawn, in spite of herself, into an old tragedy.

GENTLE TYRANT
Lucy Gillen

Working as Ross McAdam's secretary, Laura couldn't imagine why his bitchy ex-wife should see her as a rival.

DEAR CAPRICE
Juliet Gray

Clifford Fortune married Caprice but his brother, Luke, knew the marriage was a mistake. He could allow himself to love Caprice blindly but that would be betraying his own brother.

THE SONG OF THE PINES
Christina Green

Taken to a Greek island as substitute for David Nicholas's secretary, Annie quickly falls prey to the island's charms and to the charms of both Marcus, the Greek, and David himself.

GOODBYE DOCTOR GARLAND
Marjorie Harte

The story of a woman doctor who gave too much to her profession and almost lost her personal happiness.

DIGBY
Pamela Hill

Welcomed at courts throughout Europe, Kenelm Digby was the particular favourite of the Queen of France, who wanted him to be her lover, but the beautiful Venetia was the mainspring of his life.

SKINWALKERS
Tony Hillerman

The peace of the land between the sacred mountains is shattered by three murders. Is a 'skinwalker', one who has rejected the harmony of the Navajo way, the murderer?

A PARTICULAR PLACE
Mary Hocking

How is Michael Hoath, newly arrived vicar of St. Hilary's, to meet the demands of his flock and his strained marriage? Further complications follow when he falls hopelessly in love with a married parishioner.

A MATTER OF MISCHIEF
Evelyn Hood

A saga of the weaving folk in 18th century Scotland. Physician Gavin Knox was desperately seeking a cure for the pox that ravaged the slums of Glasgow and Paisley, but his adored wife, Margaret, stood in the way.

DEATH ON A HOT SUMMER NIGHT
Anne Infante

Micky Douglas is either accident-prone or someone is trying to kill him. He finds himself caught in a desperate race to save his ex-wife and others from a ruthless gang.

HOLD DOWN A SHADOW
Geoffrey Jenkins

Maluti Rider, with the help of four of the world's most wanted men, is determined to destroy the Katse Dam and release a killer flood.

THAT NICE MISS SMITH
Nigel Morland

A reconstruction and reassessment of the trial in 1857 of Madeleine Smith, who was acquitted by a verdict of Not Proven of poisoning her lover, Emile L'Angelier.

LEAVE IT TO THE HANGMAN
Bill Knox

Dope, dynamite, guns, currency — whatever it was John Kilburn and his son Pat had known how to get it in or out of England, if the price was right. But their luck changed when one of them killed a cop.

A VIOLENT END
Emma Page

To Chief Inspector Kelsey there was no shortage of suspects when Karen Boland was murdered, and that was before he discovered that she stood to inherit substantially at twenty-one.

SILENCE IN HANOVER CLOSE
Anne Perry

In 1884 Robert York is found brutally murdered at his home in Hanover Close. When, three years later, Inspector Pitt is asked to investigate, the murder remains unsolved.

THE PLEASURES OF AGE
Robert Morley

The author, British stage and screen star, now eighty, is enjoying the pleasures of age. He has drawn on his experiences to write this witty, entertaining and informative book.

THE VINEGAR SEED
Maureen Peters

The first book in a trilogy which follows the exploits of two sisters who leave Ireland in 1861 to seek their fortune in England.

A VERY PAROCHIAL MURDER
John Wainwright

A mugging in the genteel seaside town turned to murder when the victim died. Then the body of a young tearaway is washed ashore and Detective Inspector Lyle is determined that a second killing will not go unpunished.

TIGER TIGER
Frank Ryan

A young man involved in drugs is found murdered. This is the first event which will draw Detective Inspector Sandy Woodings into a whirlpool of murder and deceit.

CAROLINE MINUSCULE
Andrew Taylor

Caroline Minuscule, a medieval script, is the first clue to the whereabouts of a cache of diamonds. The search becomes a deadly kind of fairy story in which several murders have an other-worldly quality.

LONG CHAIN OF DEATH
Sarah Wolf

During the Second World War four American teenagers from the same town join the Army together. Forty-two years later, the son of one of the soldiers realises that someone is systematically wiping out the families of the four men.

A RARE BENEDICTINE
Ellis Peters

Three vintage tales of medieval intrigue and treachery featuring the author's monastic sleuth Brother Cadfael.

POIROT'S EARLY CASES
Agatha Christie

In this collection of eighteen stories, Hercule Poirot begins his celebrated career in crime.

THE SILVER LINK
— THE SILKEN LIE
Lynn Granger

Elspeth is determined to preserve her Scottish heritage and the Elliot name, but running Everanlea, a large hill farm, presents problems.

SEASONS OF MY LIFE
Hannah Hauxwell
and Barry Cockcroft

The story of Hannah Hauxwell's struggle to survive on a desolate farm in the Yorkshire Dales with little money, no electricity and no running water.

TAKING OVER
Shirley Lowe and Angela Ince

A witty insight into what happens when women take over in the boardroom and their husbands take over chores, children and chickenpox.

AFTER MIDNIGHT STORIES,
The Fourth Book Of

A collection of sixteen of the best of today's ghost stories, all different in style and approach but all combining to give the reader that special midnight shiver.